THE RANSOM OF RED CHIEF
AND OTHER O. HENRY STORIES

"*I found Bill backed up against the side of it, breathing hard, and the boy threatening to smash him with a rock half as big as a cocoanut.*"

The Ransom of Red Chief
and other
O. Henry Stories
for Boys

▼

as chosen by
FRANKLIN K. MATHIEWS

▼

GROSSET & DUNLAP, Publishers
NEW YORK
by arrangement with Doubleday Doran & Co.

PRINTED IN THE UNITED STATES
AT
THE COUNTRY LIFE PRESS, GARDEN CITY, N. Y.

CONTENTS

Contents

INTRODUCTION

Boys, meet O. Henry! That's the proper way, it seems to me, to begin an "Introduction" for you lads. As a teller of tales and spinner of yarns, by very many he is counted our country's greatest short story writer. The earlier in life you get acquainted with him, the longer you will enjoy him and the fewer will be your regrets that you didn't know him sooner. He didn't write stories for boys, but a big bunch of them might just as well have been, and after reading the ones I have chosen, you lads are likely to develop a taste for more that will make all his stories equally easy and delightful reading.

In this selection you will find stories of the wild and woolly west. Cow-punchers, Indians, desperadoes, "greasers," good men and bad aplenty, crowd one another on and off the page. As you read, one moment you will be thrilled and the very next, if you don't watch out, you will find yourself laughing so loudly you'll have to tell "what's the joke."

Above all, you boys demand the surprise, or unexpected happening in or at the end of the story. That's why you like detective stories so well. Run your eye down the table of contents and there greets you a goodly number of these, such as only O. Henry could write. Here again you will find the thrill, and again the rollicking fun to make you laugh. I promise you that, unless it be you are unlike other boys I know.

I might describe individual stories. But why should I? When the titles don't tell their own stories they so provoke your curiosity you want yourself to read the story; to tell you about it would be in part to spoil it. You want to find out for yourself what "One Dollar's Worth" is all about. And you know, of course, that "The Adventures of Shamrock Jolnes" is full of laughs, as must be "The Ransom of Red Chief."

There's another fine thing about it, too. Here's a book where it doesn't matter much whether you begin at the beginning or in the middle or at the end, it's all the same—you are bound to be immensely pleased. So, good luck to you! Perhaps some day in our travels we'll come upon each other. Should that pleasure ever be mine, I am confident you will thank me for having introduced you to O. Henry.

F. K. MATHIEWS
Chief Scout Librarian,
Boy Scouts of America.

THE RANSOM OF RED CHIEF
AND OTHER O. HENRY STORIES

THE RANSOM OF RED CHIEF AND OTHER O. HENRY STORIES

I

THE RANSOM OF RED CHIEF

IT LOOKED like a good thing: but wait till I tell you. We were down South, in Alabama —Bill Driscoll and myself—when this kidnapping idea struck us. It was, as Bill afterward expressed it, "during a moment of temporary mental apparition"; but we didn't find that out till later.

There was a town down there, as flat as a flannel-cake, and called Summit, of course. It contained inhabitants of as undeleterious and self-satisfied a class of peasantry as ever clustered around a Maypole.

Bill and me had a joint capital of about six hundred dollars, and we needed just two thousand dollars more to pull off a fraudulent town-lot scheme in Western Illinois with. We talked it over on the front steps of the

hotel. Philoprogenitiveness, says we, is
strong in semirural communities; therefore,
and for other reasons, a kidnapping project
ought to do better there than in the radius
of newspapers that send reporters out in plain
clothes to stir up talk about such things.
We knew that Summit couldn't get after us
with anything stronger than constables and,
maybe, some lackadaisical bloodhounds and
a diatribe or two in the *Weekly Farmers'
Budget*. So, it looked good.

We selected for our victim the only child of
a prominent citizen named Ebenezer Dorset.
The father was respectable and tight, a mort-
gage fancier and a stern, upright collection-
plate passer and forecloser. The kid was a
boy of ten, with bas-relief freckles, and hair
the colour of the cover of the magazine you
buy at the news-stand when you want to
catch a train. Bill and me figured that
Ebenezer would melt down for a ransom of
two thousand dollars to a cent. But wait
till I tell you.

About two miles from Summit was a little
mountain, covered with a dense cedar brake.
On the rear elevation of this mountain was a
cave. There we stored provisions.

One evening after sundown we drove in a buggy past old Dorset's house. The kid was in the street, throwing rocks at a kitten on the opposite fence.

"Hey, little boy!" says Bill, "would you like to have a bag of candy and a nice ride?"

The boy catches Bill neatly in the eye with a piece of brick.

"That will cost the old man an extra five hundred dollars," says Bill, climbing over the wheel.

That boy put up a fight like a welter-weight cinnamon bear; but, at last, we got him down in the bottom of the buggy and drove away. We took him up to the cave, and I hitched the horse in the cedar brake. After dark I drove the buggy to the little village, three miles away, where we had hired it, and walked back to the mountain.

Bill was pasting court-plaster over the scratches and bruises on his features. There was a fire burning behind the big rock at the entrance of the cave, and the boy was watching a pot of boiling coffee, with two buzzard tail-feathers stuck in his red hair. He points a stick at me when I come up, and says:

"Ha! cursed paleface, do you dare to enter the camp of Red Chief, the terror of the plains?"

"He's all right now," says Bill, rolling up his trousers and examining some bruises on his shins. "We're playing Indian. We're making Buffalo Bill's show look like magic-lantern views of Palestine in the town hall. I'm Old Hank, the Trapper, Red Chief's captive, and I'm to be scalped at daybreak. By Geronimo! that kid can kick hard."

Yes, sir, that boy seemed to be having the time of his life. The fun of camping out in a cave had made him forget that he was a captive himself. He immediately christened me Snake-eye, the Spy, and announced that, when his braves returned from the warpath, I was to be broiled at the stake at the rising of the sun.

Then we had supper; and he filled his mouth full of bacon and bread and gravy, and began to talk. He made a during-dinner speech something like this:

"I like this fine. I never camped out before; but I had a pet 'possum once, and I was nine last birthday. I hate to go to school. Rats ate up sixteen of Jimmy Talbot's aunt's speckled hen's eggs. Are there any real

Indians in these woods? I want some more gravy. Does the trees moving make the wind blow? We had five puppies. What makes your nose so red, Hank? My father has lots of money. Are the stars hot? I whipped Ed Walker twice, Saturday. I don't like girls. You dassent catch toads unless with a string. Do oxen make any noise? Why are oranges round? Have you got beds to sleep on in this cave? Amos Murray has got six toes. A parrot can talk, but a monkey or a fish can't. How many does it take to make twelve?"

Every few minutes he would remember that he was a pesky redskin, and pick up his stick rifle and tiptoe to the mouth of the cave to rubber for the scouts of the hated paleface. Now and then he would let out a warwhoop that made Old Hank the Trapper shiver. That boy had Bill terrorized from the start.

"Red Chief," says I to the kid, "would you like to go home?"

"Aw, what for?" says he. "I don't have any fun at home. I hate to go to school. I like to camp out. You won't take me back home again, Snake-eye, will you?"

"Not right away," says I. "We'll stay here in the cave awhile."

"All right!" says he. "That'll be fine. I never had such fun in all my life."

We went to bed about eleven o'clock. We spread down some wide blankets and quilts and put Red Chief between us. We weren't afraid he'd run away. He kept us awake for three hours, jumping up and reaching for his rifle and screeching: "Hist! pard," in mine and Bill's ears, as the fancied crackle of a twig or the rustle of a leaf revealed to his young imagination the stealthy approach of the outlaw band. At last I fell into a troubled sleep, and dreamed that I had been kidnapped and chained to a tree by a ferocious pirate with red hair.

Just at daybreak I was awakened by a series of awful screams from Bill. They weren't yells, or howls, or shouts, or whoops, or yawps, such as you'd expect from a manly set of vocal organs—they were simply indecent, terrifying, humiliating screams, such as women emit when they see ghosts or caterpillars. It's an awful thing to hear a strong, desperate, fat man scream incontinently in a cave at daybreak.

I jumped up to see what the matter was. Red Chief was sitting on Bill's chest, with one hand twined in Bill's hair. In the other he had the sharp case-knife we used for slicing bacon; and he was industriously and realistically trying to take Bill's scalp, according to the sentence that had been pronounced upon him the evening before.

I got the knife away from the kid and made him lie down again. But from that moment Bill's spirit was broken. He laid down on his side of the bed, but he never closed an eye again in sleep as long as that boy was with us. I dozed off for a while, but along toward sunup I remembered that Red Chief had said I was to be burned at the stake at the rising of the sun. I wasn't nervous or afraid; but I sat up and lit my pipe and leaned against a rock.

"What you getting up so soon for, Sam?" asked Bill.

"Me?" says I. "Oh, I got a kind of a pain in my shoulder. I thought sitting up would rest it."

"You're a liar!" says Bill. "You're afraid. You was to be burned at sunrise, and you was afraid he'd do it. And he would, too, if he could find a match. Ain't it awful, Sam?

Do you think anybody will pay out money to get a little imp like that back home?"

"Sure," said I. "A rowdy kid like that is just the kind that parents dote on. Now, you and the Chief get up and cook breakfast, while I go up on the top of this mountain and reconnoitre."

I went up on the peak of the little mountain and ran my eye over the contiguous vicinity. Over toward Summit I expected to see the sturdy yeomanry of the village armed with scythes and pitchforks beating the country-side for the dastardly kidnappers. But what I saw was a peaceful landscape dotted with one man ploughing with a dun mule. No-body was dragging the creek; no couriers dashed hither and yon, bringing tidings of no news to the distracted parents. There was a sylvan attitude of somnolent sleepiness per-vading that section of the external outward surface of Alabama that lay exposed to my view. "Perhaps," says I to myself, "it has not yet been discovered that the wolves have borne away the tender lambkin from the fold. Heaven help the wolves!" says I, and I went down the mountain to breakfast.

When I got to the cave I found Bill backed up against the side of it, breathing hard, and

the boy threatening to smash him with a
rock half as big as a cocoanut.

"He put a red-hot boiled potato down my
back," explained Bill, "and then mashed it with
his foot; and I boxed his ears. Have you got
a gun about you, Sam?"

I took the rock away from the boy and kind
of patched up the argument. "I'll fix you,"
says the kid to Bill. "No man ever yet
struck the Red Chief but what he got paid
for it. You better beware!"

After breakfast the kid takes a piece of
leather with strings wrapped around it out of
his pocket and goes outside the cave unwind-
ing it.

"What's he up to now?" says Bill anxiously.
"You don't think he'll run away, do you, Sam?"

"No fear of it," says I. "He don't seem
to be much of a home body. But we've got
to fix up some plan about the ransom. There
don't seem to be much excitement around
Summit on account of his disappearance: but
maybe they haven't realized yet that he's
gone. His folks may think he's spending
the night with Aunt Jane or one of the neighbours. Anyhow, he'll be missed to-day. To-
night we must get a message to his father

demanding the two thousand dollars for his return."

Just then we heard a kind of war-whoop, such as David might have emitted when he knocked out the champion Goliath. It was a sling that Red Chief had pulled out of his pocket, and he was whirling it around his head.

I dodged, and heard a heavy thud and a kind of a sigh from Bill, like a horse gives out when you take his saddle off. A niggerhead rock the size of an egg had caught Bill just behind his left ear. He loosened himself all over and fell in the fire across the frying pan of hot water for washing the dishes. I dragged him out and poured cold water on his head for half an hour.

By and by, Bill sits up and feels behind his ear and says: "Sam, do you know who my favourite Biblical character is?"

"Take it easy," says I. "You'll come to your senses presently."

"King Herod," says he. "You won't go away and leave me here alone, will you, Sam?"

I went out and caught that boy and shook him until his freckles rattled.

"If you don't behave," says I, "I'll take

you straight home.   Now, are you going to be good, or not?"

"I was only funning," says he sullenly. "I didn't mean to hurt Old Hank. But what did he hit me for? I'll behave, Snake-eye, if you won't send me home, and if you'll let me play the Black Scout to-day."

"I don't know the game," says I. "That's for you and Mr. Bill to decide. He's your playmate for the day. I'm going away for a while, on business. Now, you come in and make friends with him and say you are sorry for hurting him, or home you go, at once."

I made him and Bill shake hands, and then I took Bill aside and told him I was going to Poplar Cove, a little village three miles from the cave, and find out what I could about how the kidnapping had been regarded in Summit. Also, I thought it best to send a peremptory letter to old man Dorset that day, demanding the ransom and dictating how it should be paid.

"You know, Sam," says Bill, "I've stood by you without batting an eye in earthquakes, fire, and flood—in poker games, dynamite out-rages, police raids, train robberies, and cyclones. I never lost my nerve yet till we kidnapped that two-legged skyrocket of a kid. He's got me going. You won't leave me long with him, will you, Sam?"

"I'll be back some time this afternoon," says I. "You must keep the boy amused and quiet till I return. And now we'll write the letter to old Dorset."

Bill and I got paper and pencil and worked on the letter while Red Chief, with a blanket wrapped around him, strutted up and down, guarding the mouth of the cave. Bill begged me tearfully to make the ransom fifteen hundred dollars instead of two thousand. "I ain't attempting," says he, "to decry the celebrated moral aspect of parental affection, but we're dealing with humans, and it ain't human for anybody to give up two thousand dollars for that forty-pound chunk of freckled wildcat. I'm willing to take a chance at fifteen hundred dollars. You can charge the difference up to me."

So, to relieve Bill, I acceded, and we collaborated a letter that ran this way:

EBENEZER DORSET, ESQ.:
We have your boy concealed in a place far from Summit. It is useless for you or the most skilful detectives to attempt to find him. Absolutely, the only terms on which you can have him restored to you

are these: We demand fifteen hundred dollars in large bills for his return: the money to be left at midnight to-night at the same spot and in the same box as your reply—as hereinafter described. If you agree to these terms, send your answer in writing by a solitary messenger to-night at half-past eight o'clock. After crossing Owl Creek, on the road to Poplar Cove, there are three large trees about a hundred yards apart, close to the fence of the wheat field on the right-hand side. At the bottom of the fence-post, opposite the third tree, will be found a small pasteboard box.

The messenger will place the answer in this box and return immediately to Summit.

If you attempt any treachery or fail to comply with our demand as stated, you will never see your boy again.

If you pay the money as demanded, he will be returned to you safe and well within three hours. These terms are final, and if you do not accede to them no further communication will be attempted.

TWO DESPERATE MEN.

I addressed this letter to Dorset, and put it in my pocket. As I was about to start, the kid comes up to me and says:

"Aw, Snake-eye, you said I could play the Black Scout while you was gone."

"Play it, of course," says I. "Mr. Bill will play with you. What kind of a game is it?"

"I'm the Black Scout," says Red Chief,

"and I have to ride to the stockade to warn the settlers that the Indians are coming. I'm tired of playing Indian myself. I want to be the Black Scout."

"All right," says I. "It sounds harmless to me. I guess Mr. Bill will help you foil the pesky savages."

"What am I to do?" asks Bill, looking at the kid suspiciously.

"You are the hoss," says Black Scout. "Get down on your hands and knees. How can I ride to the stockade without a hoss?"

"You'd better keep him interested," said I, "till we get the scheme going. Loosen up."

Bill gets down on his all fours, and a look comes in his eye like a rabbit's when you catch it in a trap.

"How far is it to the stockade, kid?" he asks, in a husky manner of voice.

"Ninety miles," says the Black Scout. "And you have to hump yourself to get there on time. Whoa, now!"

The Black Scout jumps on Bill's back and digs his heels in his side.

"For Heaven's sake," says Bill, "hurry back, Sam, as soon as you can. I wish we hadn't made the ransom more than a thousand. Say, you quit kicking me or I'll get up and warm you good."

I walked over to Poplar Cove and sat around the post-office and store, talking with the chawbacons that came in to trade. One whiskerando says that he hears Summit is all upset on account of Elder Ebenezer Dorset's boy having been lost or stolen. That was all I wanted to know. I bought some smoking tobacco, referred casually to the price of black-eyed peas, posted my letter surreptitiously, and came away. The postmaster said the mail-carrier would come by in an hour to take the mail on to Summit.

When I got back to the cave Bill and the boy were not to be found. I explored the vicinity of the cave, and risked a yodel or two, but there was no response.

So I lighted my pipe and sat down on a mossy bank to wait developments.

In about half an hour I heard the bushes rustle, and Bill wabbled out into the little glade in front of the cave. Behind him was the kid, stepping softly like a scout, with a broad grin on his face. Bill stopped, took off his hat, and wiped his face with a red handkerchief. The kid stopped about eight feet behind him.

"Sam," says Bill, "I suppose you'll think I'm a renegade, but I couldn't help it. I'm a grown person with masculine proclivities and habits of self-defense, but there is a time when all systems of egotism and predominance fail. The boy is gone. I have sent him home. All is off. There was martyrs in old times," goes on Bill, "that suffered death rather than give up the particular graft they enjoyed. Ncne of 'em ever was subjugated to such supernatural tortures as I have been. I tried to be faithful to our articles of depredation; but there came a limit."

"What's the trouble, Bill?" I asks him.

"I was rode," says Bill, "the ninety miles to the stockade, not barring an inch. Then, when the settlers was rescued, I was given oats. Sand ain't a palatable substitute. And then, for an hour I had to try to explain to him why there was nothin' in holes, how a road can run both ways, and what makes the grass green. I tell you, Sam, a human can only stand so much. I takes him by the neck of his clothes and drags him down the mountain. On the way he kicks my legs

black-and-blue from the knees down; and
I've got to have two or three bites on my
thumb and hand cauterized.

"But he's gone"—continues Bill—"gone
home. I showed him the road to Summit and
kicked him about eight feet nearer there at
one kick. I'm sorry we lose the ransom; but
it was either that or Bill Driscoll to the mad-
house."

Bill is puffing and blowing, but there is a
look of ineffable peace and growing content
on his rose-pink features.

"Bill," says I, "there isn't any heart disease
in your family, is there?"

"No," says Bill, "nothing chronic except
malaria and accidents. Why?"

"Then you might turn around," says I,
"and have a look behind you."

Bill turns and sees the boy, and loses his
complexion and sits down plump on the
ground and begins to pluck aimlessly at grass
and little sticks. For an hour I was afraid
of his mind. And then I told him that my
scheme was to put the whole job through
immediately and that we would get the ransom and be off with it by midnight if old
Dorset fell in with our proposition. So Bill

braced up enough to give the kid a weak sort
of a smile and a promise to play the Russian
in a Japanese war with him as soon as he felt
a little better.

I had a scheme for collecting that ransom
without danger of being caught by counter-
plots that ought to commend itself to professional kidnappers. The tree under which
the answer was to be left—and the money
later on—was close to the road fence with big,
bare fields on all sides. If a gang of constables should be watching for any one to
come for the note they could see him a long
way off crossing the fields or in the road. But
no, sirree! At half-past eight I was up in
that tree as well hidden as a tree toad, waiting
for the messenger to arrive.

Exactly on time, a half-grown boy rides
up the road on a bicycle, locates the pasteboard box at the foot of the fence-post, slips
a folded piece of paper into it and pedals away
again back toward Summit.

I waited an hour and then concluded the
thing was square. I slid down the tree, got
the note, slipped along the fence till I struck
the woods, and was back at the cave in another half an hour. I opened the note, got

near the lantern and read it to Bill. It was written with a pen in a crabbed hand, and the sum and substance of it was this:

Two Desperate Men.

Gentlemen: I received your letter to-day by post, in regard to the ransom you ask for the return of my son. I think you are a little high in your demands, and I hereby make you a counter-proposition, which I am inclined to believe you will accept. You bring Johnny home and pay me two hundred and fifty dollars in cash, and I agree to take him off your hands. You had better come at night, for the neighbours believe he is lost, and I couldn't be responsible for what they would do to anybody they saw bringing him back.

Very respectfully,

Ebenezer Dorset.

"Great pirates of Penzance!" says I; "of all the impudent——"

But I glanced at Bill, and hesitated. He had the most appealing look in his eyes I ever saw on the face of a dumb or a talking brute.

"Sam," says he, "what's two hundred and fifty dollars, after all? We've got the money. One more night of this kid will send me to a bed in Bedlam. Besides being a thorough gentleman, I think Mr. Dorset is a spendthrift for making us such a liberal offer. **You** ain't going to let the chance go, are you?"

"Tell you the truth, Bill," says I, "this little he ewe lamb has somewhat got on my nerves, too. We'll take him home, pay the ransom, and make our get-away."

We took him home that night. We got him to go by telling him that his father had bought a silver-mounted rifle and a pair of moccasins for him, and we were going to hunt bears the next day.

It was just twelve o'clock when we knocked at Ebenezer's front door. Just at the moment when I should have been abstracting the fifteen hundred dollars from the box under the tree, according to the original proposition, Bill was counting out two hundred and fifty dollars into Dorset's hand.

When the kid found out we were going to leave him at home he started up a howl like a calliope and fastened himself as tight as a leech to Bill's leg. His father peeled him away gradually, like a porous plaster.

"How long can you hold him?" asks Bill.

"I'm not as strong as I used to be," says old Dorset, "but I think I can promise you ten minutes."

"Enough," says Bill. "In ten minutes I shall cross the Central, Southern, and Middle Western States, and be legging it trippingly for the Canadian border."

And, as dark as it was, and as fat as Bill was, and as good a runner as I am, he was a good mile and a half out of Summit before I could catch up with him.

II

JIMMY HAYES AND MURIEL

I

SUPPER was over, and there had fallen upon the camp the silence that accompanies the rolling of corn-husk cigarettes. The water-hole shone from the dark earth like a patch of fallen sky. Coyotes yelped. Dull thumps indicated the rocking-horse movements of the hobbled ponies as they moved to fresh grass. A half-troop of the Frontier Battalion of Texas Rangers were distributed about the fire.

A well-known sound—the fluttering and scraping of chaparral against wooden stir-rups—came from the thick brush above the camp. The rangers listened cautiously. They heard a loud and cheerful voice call out reassuringly:

"Brace up, Muriel, old girl, we're 'most there now! Been a long ride for ye, ain't it, ye old antediluvian handful of animated

24

carpet-tacks? Hey, now, quit a tryin' to
kiss me! Don't hold on to my neck so tight
—this here paint hoss ain't any too shore-
footed, let me tell ye. He's liable to dump us
both off if we don't watch out."

Two minutes of waiting brought a tired
"paint" pony single-footing into camp. A
gangling youth of twenty lolled in the saddle.
Of the "Muriel" whom he had been addressing, nothing was to be seen.

"Hi, fellows!" shouted the rider cheerfully.
"This here's a letter fer Lieutenant Manning."

He dismounted, unsaddled, dropped the
coils of his stake-rope, and got his hobbles
from the saddlehorn. While Lieutenant
Manning, in command, was reading the
letter, the newcomer rubbed solicitously at
some dried mud in the loops of the hobbles,
showing a consideration for the forelegs of
his mount.

"Boys," said the lieutenant, waving his
hand to the rangers, "this is Mr. James Hayes.
He's a new member of the company. Cap-
tain McLean sends him down from El Paso.
The boys will see that you have some supper,
Hayes, as soon as you get your pony hobbled."

The recruit was received cordially by the

rangers. Still, they observed him shrewdly and with suspended judgment. Picking a comrade on the border is done with ten times the care and discretion with which a girl chooses a sweetheart. On your "side-kicker's" nerve, loyalty, aim, and coolness your own life may depend many times.

After a hearty supper Hayes joined the smokers about the fire His appearance did not settle all the questions in the minds of his brother rangers. They saw simply a loose, lank youth with tow-coloured, sun-burned hair and a berry-brown, ingenuous face that wore a quizzical, good-natured smile.

"Fellows," said the new ranger, "I'm goin' to interduce to you a lady friend of mine. Ain't ever heard anybody call her a beauty, but you'll all admit she's got some fine points about her. Come along, Muriel!"

He held open the front of his blue flannel shirt. Out of it crawled a horned frog. A bright red ribbon was tied jauntily around its spiky neck. It crawled to its owner's knee and sat there, motionless.

"This here Muriel," said Hayes, with an oratorical wave of his hand, "has got qualities.

She never talks back, she always stays at home, and she's satisfied with one red dress for every day and Sunday, too."

"Look at that blame insect!" said one of the rangers with a grin. "I've seen plenty of them horny frogs, but I never knew anybody to have one for a side-partner. Does the blame thing know you from anybody else?"

"Take it over there and see," said Hayes.

The stumpy little lizard known as the horned frog is harmless. He has the hideousness of the prehistoric monsters whose reduced descendant he is, but he is gentler than the dove.

The ranger took Muriel from Hayes's knee and went back to his seat on a roll of blankets. The captive twisted and clawed and struggled vigorously in his hand. After holding it for a moment or two, the ranger set it upon the ground. Awkwardly but swiftly the frog worked its four oddly moving legs until it stopped close by Hayes's foot.

"Well, dang my hide!" said the other ranger. "The little cuss knows you. Never thought them insects had that much sense!"

II

Jimmy Hayes became a favourite in the
ranger camp. He had an endless store of
good nature, and a mild, perennial quality
of humour that is well adapted to camp life.
He was never without his horned frog. In
the bosom of his shirt during rides, on his
knee or shoulder in camp, under his blankets
at night, the ugly little beast never left him.

Jimmy was a humourist of a type that pre-
vails in the rural South and West. Unskilled
in originating methods of amusing or in witty
conceptions, he had hit upon a comical idea
and clung to it reverently. It had seemed
to Jimmy a very funny thing to have about
his person, with which to amuse his friends,
a tame horned frog with a red ribbon around
its neck. As it was a happy idea, why not
perpetuate it?

The sentiments existing between Jimmy and
the frog cannot be exactly determined. The
capability of the horned frog for lasting affection is a subject upon which we have had
no symposiums. It is easier to guess Jimmy's
feelings. Muriel was his *chef d'œuvre* of wit,.

and as such he cherished her. He caught
flies for her, and shielded her from sudden
northers. Yet his care was half selfish, and
when the time came she repaid him a thousand
fold. Other Muriels have thus overbalanced
the light attentions of other Jimmies.

Not at once did Jimmy Hayes attain full
brotherhood with his comrades. They loved
him for his simplicity and drollness, but there
hung above him a great sword of suspended
judgment. To make merry in camp is not
all of a ranger's life. There are horse-thieves
to trail, desperate criminals to run down,
bravos to battle with, bandits to rout out of
the chaparral, peace and order to be com-
pelled at the muzzle of a six-shooter. Jimmy
had been " 'most generally a cow-puncher,"
he said; he was inexperienced in ranger
methods of warfare. Therefore the ranger
speculated apart and solemnly as to how he
would stand fire. For, let it be known, the
honour and pride of each ranger company is
the individual bravery of its members.

For two months the border was quiet. The
rangers lolled, listless, in camp. And then—
bringing joy to the rusting guardians of the
frontier—Sebastiano Saldar, an eminent Mex-

ican desperado and cattle-thief, crossed the Rio Grande with his gang and began to lay waste the Texas side. There were indications that Jimmy Hayes would soon have the opportunity to show his mettle. The rangers patrolled with alacrity, but Saldar's men were mounted like Lochinvar, and were hard to catch.

One evening, about sundown, the rangers halted for supper after a long ride. Their horses stood panting, with their saddles on. The men were frying bacon and boiling coffee. Suddenly, out of the brush, Sebastiano Saldar and his gang dashed upon them with blazing six-shooters and high-voiced yells. It was a neat surprise. The rangers swore in annoyed tones, and got their Winchesters busy; but the attack was only a spectacular dash of the purest Mexican type. After the florid demonstration the raiders galloped away, yelling, down the river. The rangers mounted and pursued; but in less than two miles the fagged ponies laboured so that Lieutenant Manning gave the word to abandon the chase and return to the camp.

Then it was discovered that Jimmy Hayes was missing. Some one remembered having

seen him run for his pony when the attack
began, but no one had set eyes on him since.
Morning came, but no Jimmy. They searched
the country around, on the theory that he
had been killed or wounded, but without success. Then they followed after Saldar's gang,
but it seemed to have disappeared. Manning
concluded that the wily Mexican had re-
crossed the river after his theatric farewell.
And, indeed, no further depredations from him
were reported.

This gave the rangers time to nurse a sore-
ness they had. As has been said, the pride
and honour of the company is the individual
bravery of its members. And now they believed that Jimmy Hayes had turned coward
at the whiz of Mexican bullets. There was
no other deduction. Buck Davis pointed
out that not a shot was fired by Saldar's
gang after Jimmy was seen running for his
horse. There was no way for him to have
been shot. No, he had fled from his first
fight, and afterward he would not return,
aware that the scorn of his comrades would be
a worse thing to face than the muzzles of
many rifles.

So Manning's detachment of McLean's

company, Frontier Battalion, was gloomy.
It was the first blot on its escutcheon. Never
before in the history of the service had a
ranger shown the white feather. All of them
had liked Jimmy Hayes, and that made it
worse.

Days, weeks, and months went by, and
still that little cloud of unforgotten cowardice
hung above the camp.

III

Nearly a year afterward—after many camping grounds and many hundreds of miles
guarded and defended—Lieutenant Manning,
with almost the same detachment of men,
was sent to a point only a few miles below
their old camp on the river to look after some
smuggling there. One afternoon, while they
were riding through a dense mesquite flat,
they came upon a patch of open hog-wallow
prairie. There they rode upon the scene of an
unwritten tragedy.

In a big hog-wallow lay the skeletons of
three Mexicans. Their clothing alone served
to identify them. The largest of the figures
had once been Sebastiano Saldar. His great,
costly sombrero, heavy with gold ornamenta-

tion—a hat famous all along the Rio Grande—
lay there pierced by three bullets. Along
the ridge of the hog-wallow rested the rusting
Winchester of the Mexicans—all pointing in
the same direction.

The rangers rode in that direction for fifty
yards. There, in a little depression of the
ground, with his rifle still bearing upon the
three, lay another skeleton. It had been a
battle of extermination. There was nothing
to identify the solitary defender. His clothing—such as the elements had left distin-
guishable—seemed to be of the kind that any
ranchman or cowboy might have worn.

"Some cow-puncher," said Manning, "that
they caught out alone. Good boy! He put
up a dandy scrap before they got him. So
that's why we didn't hear from Don Sebastiano any more!"

And then, from beneath the weather-
beaten rags of the dead man, there wriggled
out a horned frog with a faded red ribbon
around its neck, and sat upon the shoulder
of its long quiet master. Mutely it told
the story of the untried youth and the swift
"paint" pony—how they had outstripped all
their comrades that day in the pursuit of the

Mexican raiders. and how the boy had gone down upholding the honour of the company.

The ranger troop herded close, and a simultaneous wild yell arose from their lips. The outburst was at once a dirge, an apology, an epitaph, and a pæan of triumph. A strange requiem, you may say, over the body of a fallen comrade; but if Jimmy Hayes could have heard it he would have understood.

III

A TECHNICAL ERROR

I NEVER cared especially for feuds, believing them to be even more overrated products of our country than grapefruit, scrapple, or honeymoons. Nevertheless, if I may be allowed, I will tell you of an Indian Territory feud of which I was press-agent, camp-follower, and inaccessory during the fact.

I was on a visit to Sam Durkee's ranch, where I had a great time falling off unmanicured ponies and waving my bare hand at the lower jaws of wolves about two miles away. Sam was a hardened person of about twenty-five, with a reputation for going home in the dark with perfect equanimity, though often with reluctance.

Over in the Creek Nation was a family bearing the name of Tatum. I was told that the Durkees and Tatums had been feuding for years. Several of each family had bitten the grass, and it was expected that more

Nebuchadnezzars would follow. A younger generation of each family was growing up, and the grass was keeping pace with them. But I gathered that they had fought fairly; that they had not lain in cornfields and aimed at the division of their enemies' suspenders in the back—partly, perhaps, because there were no cornfields, and nobody wore more than one suspender. Nor had any woman or child of either house ever been harmed. In those days—and you will find it so yet—their women were safe.

Sam Durkee had a girl. (If it were an all-fiction magazine that I expect to sell this story to, I should say, "Mr. Durkee rejoiced in a fiancée.") Her name was Ella Baynes. They appeared to be devoted to each other, and to have perfect confidence in each other, as all couples do who are and have or aren't and haven't. She was tolerably pretty, with a heavy mass of brown hair that helped her along. He introduced me to her, which seemed not to lessen her preference for him; so I reasoned that they were surely soul mates.

Miss Baynes lived in Kingfisher, twenty miles from the ranch. Sam lived on a gallop between the two places.

One day there came to Kingfisher a courageous young man, rather small, with smooth face and regular features. He made many inquiries about the business of the town, and especially of the inhabitants cognominally. He said he was from Muscogee, and he looked it, with his yellow shoes and crocheted four-in-hand. I met him once when I rode in for the mail. He said his name was Beverly Travers, which seemed rather improbable.

There were active times on the ranch, just then, and Sam was too busy to go to town often. As an incompetent and generally worthless guest, it devolved upon me to ride in for little things such as post cards, barrels of flour, baking-powder, smoking-tobacco, and —letters from Ella.

One day, when I was messenger for half a gross of cigarette papers and a couple of wagon tires, I saw the alleged Beverly Travers in a yellow-wheeled buggy with Ella Baynes, driving about town as ostentatiously as the black, waxy mud would permit. I knew that this information would bring no balm of Gilead to Sam's soul, so I refrained from including it in the news of the city that I retailed on my return. But on the next

afternoon an elongated ex-cowboy of the
name of Simmons, an oldtime pal of Sam's
who kept a feed store in Kingfisher, rode
out to the ranch and rolled and burned many
cigarettes before he would talk. When he
did make oration, his words were these:

"Say, Sam, there's been a description of a
galoot miscallin' himself Bevel-edged Travels
impairing the atmospheric air of Kingfisher
for the past two weeks. You know who he
was? He was not otherwise than Ben Tatum,
from the Creek Nation, son of old Gopher
Tatum that your Uncle Newt shot last
February. You know what he done this
morning? He killed your brother Lester—
shot him in the co't-house yard."

I wonder if Sam had heard. He pulled a
twig from a mesquite bush, chewed it gravely,
and said:

"He did, did he? He killed Lester?"

"The same," said Simmons. "And he did
more. He run away with your girl, the
same as to say Miss Ella Baynes. I thought
you might like to know, so I rode out to
impart the information."

"I am much obliged, Jim," said Sam,
taking the chewed twig from his mouth.

"Yes, I'm glad you rode out. Yes, I'm right glad."

"Well, I'll be ridin' back, I reckon. That boy I left in the feed store don't know hay from oats. He shot Lester in the *back*."

"Shot him in the back?"

"Yes, while he was hitchin' his hoss."

"I'm much obliged, Jim."

"I kind of thought you'd like to know as soon as you could."

"Come in and have some coffee before you ride back, Jim?"

"Why, no, I reckon not; I must get back to the store."

"And you say——"

"Yes, Sam. Everybody seen 'em drive away together in a buckboard, with a big bundle, like clothes, tied up in the back of it. He was drivin' the team he brought over with him from Muscogee. They'll be hard to overtake right away."

"And which——"

"I was goin' on to tell you. They left on the Guthrie road; but there's no tellin' which forks they'll take—you know that."

"All right, Jim; much obliged."

"You're welcome, Sam."

Simmons rolled a cigarette and stabbed his pony with both heels. Twenty yards away he reined up and called back:

"You don't want no—assistance, as you might say?"

"Not any, thanks."

"I didn't think you would. Well, so long!"

Sam took out and opened a bone-handled pocket-knife and scraped a dried piece of mud from his left boot. I thought at first he was going to swear a vendetta on the blade of it, or recite "The Gipsy's Curse." The few feuds I had ever seen or read about usually opened that way. This one seemed to be presented with a new treatment. Thus offered on the stage, it would have been hissed off, and one of Belasco's thrilling melodramas demanded instead.

"I wonder," said Sam, with a profoundly thoughtful expression, "if the cook has any cold beans left over!"

He called Wash, the Negro cook, and finding that he had some, ordered him to heat up the pot and make some strong coffee. Then we went into Sam's private room, where he slept, and kept his armoury, dogs, and the saddles of his favourite mounts. He took three or four six-shooters out of a bookcase and began to look them over, whistling "The Cowboy's Lament" abstractedly. Afterward he ordered the two best horses on the ranch saddled and tied to the hitching-post.

Now, in the feud business, in all sections of the country, I have observed that in one particular there is a delicate but strict etiquette belonging. You must not mention the word or refer to the subject in the presence of a feudist. It would be more reprehensible than commenting upon the mole on the chin of your rich aunt. I found, later on, that there is another unwritten rule, but I think that belongs solely to the West.

It yet lacked two hours to supper-time; but in twenty minutes Sam and I were plunging deep into the reheated beans, hot coffee, and cold beef.

"Nothing like a good meal before a long ride," said Sam. "Eat hearty."

I had a sudden suspicion.

"Why did you have two horses saddled?" I asked.

"One, two—one, two," said Sam. "You can count, can't you?"

His mathematics carried with it a momentary qualm and a lesson. The thought had not occurred to him that the thought could possibly occur to me not to ride at his side on that red road to revenge and justice. It was the higher calculus. I was booked for the trail. I began to eat more beans.

In an hour we set forth at a steady gallop eastward. Our horses were Kentucky-bred, strengthened by the mesquite grass of the west. Ben Tatum's steeds may have been swifter, and he had a good lead, but if he had heard the punctual thuds of the hoofs of those trailers of ours, born in the heart of feudland, he might have felt that retribution was creeping up on the hoof-prints of his dapper nags.

I knew that Ben Tatum's card to play was flight—flight until he came within the safe territory of his own henchmen and supporters. He knew that the man pursuing him would follow the trail to any end where it might lead.

During the ride Sam talked of the prospect for rain, of the price of beef, and of the musical glasses. You would have thought he had never had a brother or a sweetheart or an enemy on earth. There are some sub-

jects too big even for the words in the "Unabridged." Knowing this phase of the feud
code, but not having practised it sufficiently,
I overdid the thing by telling some slightly
funny anecdotes. Sam laughed at exactly the
right place—laughed with his mouth. When
I caught sight of his mouth, I wished I had
been blessed with enough sense of humour to
have suppressed those anecdotes.

Our first sight of them we had in Guthrie.
Tired and hungry, we stumbled, unwashed,
into a little yellow-pine hotel and sat at a
table. In the opposite corner we saw the
fugitives. They were bent upon their meal,
but looked around at times uneasily.

The girl was dressed in brown—one of
these smooth, half-shiny, silky-looking affairs
with lace collar and cuffs, and what I believe
they call an accordion-plaited skirt. She
wore a thick brown veil down to her nose,
and a broad-brimmed straw hat with some
kind of feathers adorning it. The man wore
plain, dark clothes, and his hair was trimmed
very short. He was such a man as you
might see anywhere.

There they were—the murderer and the
woman he had stolen. There we were—the

rightful avenger, according to the code, and the supernumerary who writes these words.

For one time, at least, in the heart of the supernumerary there rose the killing instinct. For one moment he joined the force of combatants—orally.

"What are you waiting for, Sam?" I said in a whisper. "Let him have it now!"

Sam gave a melancholy sigh.

"You don't understand; but *he* does," he said. "*He* knows. Mr. Tenderfoot, there's a rule out here among white men in the Nation that you can't shoot a man when he's with a woman. I never knew it to be broke yet. You *can't* do it. You've got to get him in a gang of men or by himself. That's why. He knows it, too. We all know. So, that's Mr. Ben Tatum! One of the 'pretty men'! I'll cut him out of the herd before they leave the hotel, and regulate his account!"

After supper the flying pair disappeared quickly. Although Sam haunted lobby and stairway and halls half the night, in some mysterious way the fugitives eluded him; and in the morning the veiled lady in the brown dress with the accordion-plaited skirt and the dapper young man with the close-clipped hair, and the buckboard with the prancing nags, were gone.

It is a monotonous story, that of the ride; so it shall be curtailed. Once again we overtook them on a road. We were about fifty yards behind. They turned in the buckboard and looked at us; then drove on without whipping up their horses. Their safety no longer lay in speed. Ben Tatum knew. He knew that the only rock of safety left to him was the code. There is no doubt that, had he been alone, the matter would have been settled quickly with Sam Durkee in the usual way; but he had something at his side that kept still the trigger-finger of both. It seemed likely that he was no coward.

So, you may perceive that woman, on occasions, may postpone instead of precipitating conflict between man and man. But not willingly or consciously. She is oblivious of codes.

Five miles farther we came upon the future great Western city of Chandler. The horses of pursuers and pursued were starved and weary. There was one hotel that offered danger to man and entertainment to beast;

so the four of us met again in the dining room
at the ringing of a bell so resonant and large
that it had cracked the welkin long ago. The
dining room was not as large as the one at
Guthrie.

Just as we were eating apple pie—how Ben
Davises and tragedy impinge upon each
other!—I noticed Sam looking with keen
intentness at our quarry where they were
seated at a table across the room. The girl
still wore the brown dress with lace collar
and cuffs, and the veil drawn down to her
nose. The man bent over his plate, with his
close-cropped head held low.

"There's a code," I heard Sam say, either
to me or to himself, "that won't let you
shoot a man in the company of a woman;
but, by thunder, there ain't one to keep you
from killing a woman in the company of a
man!"

And, quicker than my mind could follow
his argument, he whipped a Colt's automatic
from under his left arm and pumped six
bullets into the body that the brown dress
covered—the brown dress with the lace collar
and cuffs and the accordion-plaited skirt.

The young person in the dark sack suit,

from whose head and from whose life a woman's glory had been clipped, laid her head on her arms stretched upon the table; while people came running to raise Ben Tatum from the floor in his feminine masquerade that had given Sam the opportunity to set aside, technically, the obligations of the code.

IV

THE REFORMATION OF CALLIOPE

CALLIOPE CATESBY was in his humours again. Ennui was upon him. This goodly promontory, the earth—particularly that portion of it known as Quicksand—was to him no more than a pestilent congregation of favours. Overtaken by the megrims, the philosopher may seek relief in soliloquy; my lady find solace in tears; the flaccid Easterner scold at the millinery bills of his women folk. Such recourse was insufficient to the denizens of Quicksand. Calliope, especially, was wont to express his ennui according to his lights.

Over night Calliope had hung out signals of approaching low spirits. He had kicked his own dog on the porch of the Occidental Hotel, and refused to apologise. He had become capricious and fault-finding in conversation. While strolling about he reached often for twigs of mesquite and chewed the

leaves fiercely. That was always an ominous
act. Another symptom alarming to those
who were familiar with the different stages
of his doldrums was his increasing politeness
and a tendency to use formal phrases. A
husky softness succeeded the usual penetrat-
ing drawl in his tones. A dangerous courtesy
marked his manners. Later, his smile became crooked, the left side of his mouth slant-
ing upward, and Quicksand got ready to
stand from under.

At this stage Calliope generally began to
drink. Finally, about midnight, he was seen
going homeward, saluting those whom he
met with exaggerated but inoffensive courtesy.
Not yet was Calliope's melancholy at the
danger point. He would seat himself at the
window of the room he occupied over Silves-
ter's tonsorial parlours and there chant lu-
gubrious and tuneless ballads until morning,
accompanying the noises by appropriate mal-
treatment of a jingling guitar. More magnanimous than Nero, he would thus give
musical warning of the forthcoming municipal upheaval that Quicksand was scheduled
to endure.

A quiet, amiable man was Calliope Catesby

at other times—quiet to indolence, and amiable to worthlessness.   At best he was a loafer and a nuisance; at worst he was the Terror of Quicksand.   His ostensible occupation was something subordinate in the real estate line; he drove the beguiled Easterner in buckboards out to look over lots and ranch property.   Originally he came from one of the Gulf States, his lank six feet, slurring rhythm of speech, and sectional idioms giving evidence of his birthplace.

And yet, after taking on Western adjustments, this languid pine-box whittler, cracker-barrel hugger, shady corner lounger of the cotton fields and sumac hills of the South became famed as a bad man among men who had made a life-long study of the art of truculence.

At nine the next morning Calliope was fit. Inspired by his own barbarous melodies and the contents of his jug, he was ready primed to gather fresh laurels from the diffident brow of Quicksand. Encircled and crisscrossed with cartridge belts, abundantly garnished with revolvers, and copiously drunk, he poured forth into Quicksand's main street. Too chivalrous to surprise and capture a

town by silent sortie, he paused at the nearest
corner and emitted his slogan—that fearful,
brassy yell, so reminiscent of the steam piano,
that had gained for him the classic appellation
that had superseded his own baptismal name.
Following close upon his vociferation came
three shots from his forty-five by way of lim-
bering up the guns and testing his aim. A
yellow dog, the personal property of Colonel
Swazey, the proprietor of the Occidental, fell
feet upward in the dust with one farewell yelp.
A Mexican who was crossing the street from
the Blue Front grocery, carrying in his hand a
bottle of kerosene, was stimulated to a sudden
and admirable burst of speed, still grasping
the neck of the shattered bottle. The new
gilt weathercock on Judge Riley's lemon and
ultramarine two-story residence shivered, flap-
ped, and hung by a splinter, the sport of the
wanton breezes.

  The artillery was in trim. Calliope's hand
was steady. The high, calm ecstasy of habitual battle was upon him, though slightly
embittered by the sadness of Alexander in
that his conquests were limited to the small
world of Quicksand.

Down the street went Calliope, shooting

right and left. Glass fell like hail; dogs
vamosed; chickens flew, squawking; feminine
voices shrieked concernedly to youngsters at
large. The din was perforated at intervals
by the *staccato* of the Terror's guns, and was
drowned periodically by the brazen screech
that Quicksand knew so well. The occasions
of Calliope's low spirits were legal holidays in
Quicksand. All along the main street in
advance of his coming clerks were putting up
shutters and closing doors. Business would
languish for a space. The right of way was
Calliope's, and as he advanced, observing the
dearth of opposition and the few opportunities
for distraction, his ennui perceptibly increased.

But some four squares farther down lively
preparations were being made to minister to
Mr. Catesby's love for interchange of compliments and repartee. On the previous night
numerous messengers had hastened to advise
Buck Patterson, the city marshal, of Calliope's
impending eruption. The patience of that
official, often strained in extending leniency
toward the disturber's misdeeds, had been
overtaxed. In Quicksand some indulgence was
accorded the natural ebullition of human
nature. Providing that the lives of the more

useful citizens were not recklessly squandered, or too much property needlessly laid waste, the community sentiment was against a too strict enforcement of the law. But Calliope had raised the limit. His outbursts had been too frequent and too violent to come within the classification of a normal and sanitary relaxation of spirit.

Buck Patterson had been expecting and awaiting in his little ten-by-twelve frame office that preliminary yell announcing that Calliope was feeling blue. When the signal came the City Marshal rose to his feet and buckled on his guns. Two deputy sheriffs and three citizens who had proven the edible qualities of fire also stood up, ready to bandy with Calliope's leaden jocularities.

"Gather that fellow in," said Buck Patterson, setting forth the lines of the campaign. "Don't have no talk, but shoot as soon as you can get a show. Keep behind cover and bring him down. He's a nogood 'un. It's up to Calliope to turn up his toes this time, I reckon. Go to him all spraddled out, boys. And don't git too reckless, for what Calliope shoots at he hits."

Buck Patterson, tall, muscular, and solemn-faced, with his bright "City Marshal" badge shining on the breast of his blue flannel shirt, gave his posse directions for the onslaught upon Calliope. The plan was to accomplish the downfall of the Quicksand Terror without loss to the attacking party, if possible.

The splenetic Calliope, unconscious of retributive plots, was steaming down the channel, cannonading on either side, when he suddenly became aware of breakers ahead. The city marshal and one of the deputies rose up behind some dry-goods boxes half a square to the front and opened fire. At the same time the rest of the posse, divided, shelled him from two side streets up which they were cautiously manœuvring from a well-executed detour.

The first volley broke the lock of one of Calliope's guns, cut a neat underbit in his right ear, and exploded a cartridge in his crossbelt, scorching his ribs as it burst. Feeling braced up by this unexpected tonic to his spiritual depression, Calliope executed a fortissimo note from his upper register, and returned the fire like an echo. The upholders of the law dodged at his flash, but a trifle too late to save one of the deputies a bullet just above the elbow, and the marshal a bleeding cheek from a splinter that a ball tore from the box he had ducked behind.

And now Calliope met the enemy's tactics in kind. Choosing with a rapid eye the street from which the weakest and least accurate fire had come, he invaded it at a double-quick, abandoning the unprotected middle of the street. With rare cunning the opposing force in that direction—one of the deputies and two of the valorous volunteers—waited, concealed by beer barrels, until Calliope had passed their retreat, and then peppered him from the rear. In another moment they were reinforced by the marshal and his other men, and then Calliope felt that in order to successfully prolong the delights of the controversy he must find some means of reducing the great odds against him. His eye fell upon a structure that seemed to hold out this promise, providing he could reach it.

Not far away was the little railroad station, its building a strong box house, ten by twenty feet, resting upon a platform four feet above ground. Windows were in each of its walls. Something like a fort it might become to a man thus sorely pressed by superior numbers.

Calliope made a bold and rapid spurt for it, the marshal's crowd "smoking" him as he ran. He reached the haven in safety, the station agent leaving the building by a window, like a flying squirrel, as the garrison entered the door.

Patterson and his supporters halted under protection of a pile of lumber and held consultations. In the station was an unterrified desperado who was an excellent shot and carried an abundance of ammunition. For thirty yards on each side of the besieged was a stretch of bare, open ground. It was a sure thing that the man who attempted to enter that unprotected area would be stopped by one of Calliope's bullets.

The city marshal was resolved. He had decided that Calliope Catesby should no more wake the echoes of Quicksand with his strident whoop. He had so announced. Officially and personally he felt imperatively bound to put the soft pedal on that instrument of discord. It played bad tunes.

Standing near was a hand truck used in the manipulation of small freight. It stood by a shed full of sacked wool, a consignment from one of the sheep ranches. On this truck the

marshal and his men piled three heavy sacks
of wool. Stooping low, Buck Patterson started
for Calliope's fort, slowly pushing this loaded
truck before him for protection. The posse,
scattering broadly, stood ready to nip the
besieged in case he should show himself in an
effort to repel the juggernaut of justice that
was creeping upon him. Only once did Calliope make demonstration. He fired from a
window, and some tufts of wool spurted from
the marshal's trustworthy bulwark. The return shots from the posse pattered against
the window frame of the fort. No loss re-
sulted on either side.

The marshal was too deeply engrossed in
steering his protected battleship to be aware
of the approach of the morning train until
he was within a few feet of the platform.
The train was coming up on the other side
of it. It stopped only one minute at Quicksand. What an opportunity it would offer
to Calliope! He had only to step out the
other door, mount the train, and away.

Abandoning his breastworks, Buck, with
his gun ready, dashed up the steps and into
the room, driving open the closed door with
one heave of his weighty shoulder. The

members of the posse heard one shot fired in-side, and then there was silence.

At length the wounded man opened his eyes. After a blank space he again could see and hear and feel and think. Turning his eyes about, he found himself lying on a wooden bench. A tall man with a perplexed countenance, wearing a big badge with "City Marshal" engraved upon it, stood over him. A little old woman in black, with a wrinkled face and sparkling black eyes, was holding a wet handkerchief against one of his temples. He was trying to get these facts fixed in his mind and connected with past events, when the old woman began to talk.

"There now, great, big, strong man! That bullet never teched ye! Jest skeeted along the side of your head and sort of paralyzed ye for a spell. I've heerd of secl things afore; cun-cussion is what they names it. Abel Wadkins used to kill squirrels that way— barkin' em, Abe called it. You jest been barked, sir, and you'll be all right in a little bit. Feel lots better already, don't ye! You just lay still a while longer and let me bathe your head. You don't know me, I reckon, and 'tain't surprisin' that you shouldn't. I

come in on that train from Alabama to see my
son. Big son, ain't he? Lands! you wouldn't
hardly think he'd ever been a baby, would ye?
This is my son, sir."

Half turning, the old woman looked up
at the standing man, her worn face lighting
with a proud and wonderful smile. She
reached out one veined and calloused hand
and took one of her son's. Then smiling
cheerily down at the prostrate man, she continued to dip the handkerchief in the waiting-
room tin washbasin and gently apply it to
his temple. She had the benevolent garrulity
of old age.

"I ain't seen my son before," she continued,
"in eight years. One of my nephews, El-
kanah Price, he's a conductor on one of them
railroads and he got me a pass to come out
here. I can stay a whole week on it, and
then it'll take me back again. Jest think,
now, that little boy of mine has got to be a
officer—a city marshal of a whole town!
That's somethin' like a constable, ain't it?
I never knowed he was a officer: he didn't
say nothin' about it in his letters. I reckon
he thought his old mother'd be skeered about
the danger he was in. But, laws! I never

was much of a hand to git skeered. 'Tain't
no use. I heard them guns a-shootin' while
I was gittin' off them cars, and I see smoke a-
comin' out of the depot, but I jest walked
right along. Then I see son's face lookin'
out through the window. I knowed him at
oncet. He met me at the door, and squeezed
me 'most to death. And there you was, sir,
a-lyin' there jest like you was dead, and I
'lowed we'd see what might be done to help
sot you up."

"I think I'll sit up now," said the concussion
patient. "I'm feeling pretty fair by this time."

He sat, somewhat weakly yet, leaning
against the wall. He was a rugged man, big-
boned and straight. His eyes, steady and
keen, seemed to linger upon the face of the
man standing so still above him. His look
wandered often from the face he studied to
the marshal's badge upon the other's breast.

"Yes, yes, you'll be all right," said the old
woman, patting his arm, "if you don't get to
cuttin' up agin, and havin' folks shootin'
at you. Son told me about you, sir, while
you was layin' senseless on the floor. Don't
you take it as meddlesome fer an old woman
with a son as big as you to talk about it.

And you mustn't hold no grudge ag'in my
son for havin' to shoot at ye. A officer has
got to take up for the law—it's his duty
—and them that acts bad and lives wrong
has to suffer. Don't blame my son any, sir
—'tain't his fault. He's always been a good
boy—good when he was growin' up, and
kind and 'bedient and well-behaved. Won't
you let me advise you, sir, not to do so no
more? Be a good man, and leave liquor
alone and live peaceably and godly. Keep
away from bad company and work honest
and sleep sweet."

The black-mittened hand of the old pleader
gently touched the breast of the man she addressed. Very earnest and candid her old,
worn face looked. In her rusty black dress
and antique bonnet she sat, near the close of
a long life, and epitomized the experience of
the world. Still the man to whom she spoke
gazed above her head, contemplating the silent
son of the old mother.

"What does the marshal say?" he asked.
"Does he believe the advice is good? Suppose the marshal speaks up and says if the
talk's all right?"

The tall man moved uneasily. He fingered

the badge on his breast for a moment, and then he put an arm around the old woman and drew her close to him. She smiled the unchanging mother smile of three-score years, and patted his big brown hand with her crooked, mittened fingers while her son spake.

"I says this," he said, looking squarely into the eyes of the other man, "that if I was in your place I'd follow it. If I was a drunken, desp'rate character, without shame or hope, I'd follow it. If I was in your place and you was in mine I'd say: 'Marshal, I'm willin' to swear if you'll give me the chance I'll quit the racket. I'll drop the tanglefoot and the gun-play, and won't play hoss no more. I'll be a good citizen and go to work and quit my foolishness. So help me God!' That's what I'd say to you if you was marshal and I was in your place.'"

"Hear my son talkin'," said the old woman softly. "Hear him, sir. You promise to be good and he won't do you no harm. Forty-one year ago his heart first beat ag'in' mine, and it's beat true ever since."

The other man rose to his feet, trying his limbs and stretching his muscles.

"Then," said he, "if you was in my place

and said that, and I was marshal, I'd say:
'Go free, and do your best to keep your
promise.'"

"Lawsy!" exclaimed the old woman, in a
sudden flutter, "ef I didn't clear forget that
trunk of mine!   I see a man settin' it on the
platform jest as I seen son's face in the window, and it went plum out of my head.
There's eight jars of home-made quince jam
in that trunk that I made myself.   I wouldn't
have nothin' happen to them jars for a red
apple."

Away to the door she trotted, spry and
anxious, and then Calliope Catesby spoke out
to Buck Patterson:

"I just couldn't help it, Buck.   I seen her
through the window a-comin' in.   She never
had heard a word 'bout my tough ways.   I
didn't have the nerve to let her know I was
a worthless cuss bein' hunted down by the
community.   There you was lyin' where my
shot laid you, like you was dead.   The idea
struck me sudden, and I just took your badge
off and fastened it onto myself, and I fastened
my reputation onto you.   I told her I was the
marshal and you was a holy terror.   You can
take your badge back now, Buck."

With shaking fingers Calliope began to unfasten the disc of metal from his shirt.

"Easy there!" said Buck Patterson. "You keep that badge right where it is, Calliope Catesby. Don't you dare to take it off till the day your mother leaves this town. You'll be city marshal of Quicksand as long as she's here to know it. After I stir around town a bit and put 'em on I'll guarantee that nobody won't give the thing away to her. And say, you leather-headed, rip-roarin', low-down son of a locoed cyclone, you follow that advice she give me! I'm goin' to take some of it myself, too."

"Buck," said Calliope feelingly, "ef I don't I hope I may——"

"Shut up," said Buck. "She's a-comin' back."

V

JEFF PETERS AS A PERSONAL MAGNET

JEFF PETERS has been engaged in as many schemes for making money as there are recipes for cooking rice in Charleston, S. C.

Best of all I like to hear him tell of his earlier days when he sold liniments and cough cures on street corners, living hand to mouth, heart to heart with the people, throwing heads or tails with fortune for his last coin.

"I struck Fisher Hill, Arkansaw," said he, "in a buckskin suit, moccasins, long hair, and a thirty-carat diamond ring that I got from an actor in Texarkana. I don't know what he ever did with the pocket knife I swapped him for it.

"I was Doctor Waugh-hoo, the celebrated Indian medicine man. I carried only one best bet just then, and that was Resurrection Bitters. It was made of life-giving plants and herbs accidentally discovered by Ta-qua-la, the beautiful wife of the chief of the Choctaw Nation, while gathering truck to garnish a platter of boiled dog for the annual corn dance.

"Business hadn't been good at the last town, so I only had five dollars. I went to the Fisher Hill druggist and he credited me for half a gross of eight-ounce bottles and corks. I had the labels and ingredients in my valise, left over from the last town. Life began to look rosy again after I got in my hotel room with the water running from the tap, and the Resurrection Bitters lining up on the table by the dozen.

"Fake? No, sir. There was two dollars' worth of fluid extract of cinchona and a dime's worth of aniline in that half-gross of bitters. I've gone through towns years afterwards and had folks ask for 'em again.

"I hired a wagon that night and commenced selling the bitters on Main Street. Fisher Hill was a low, malarial town; and a compound hypothetical pneumo-cardiac anti-scorbutic tonic was just what I diagnosed the crowd as needing. The bitters started off like sweetbreads-on-toast at a vegetarian dinner. I had sold two dozen at fifty cents apiece when I felt somebody pull my coat tail. I knew what that meant; so I climbed down and sneaked a

five-dollar bill into the hand of a man with a
German silver star on his lapel.

"'Constable,' says I, 'it's a fine night.'

"'Have you got a city license,' he asks, 'to
sell this illegitimate essence of spooju that you
flatter by the name of medicine?'

"'I have not,' says I. 'I didn't know you
had a city. If I can find it to-morrow I'll take
one out if it's necessary.'

"'I'll have to close you up till you do,' says
the constable.

"I quit selling and went back to the hotel.
I was talking to the landlord about it.

"'Oh, you won't stand no show in Fisher
Hill,' says he. 'Doctor Hoskins, the only
doctor here, is a brother-in-law of the Mayor,
and they won't allow no fake doctor to practice in town.'

"'I don't practice medicine,' says I, 'I've
got a State peddler's license, and I take out a
city one wherever they demand it.'

"I went to the Mayor's office the next
morning and they told me he hadn't showed
up yet. They didn't know when he'd be
down. So Doc Waugh-hoo hunches down
again in a hotel chair and lights a jimpson-
weed regalia, and waits.

"By and by a young man in a blue necktie slips into the chair next to me and asks the time.

"'Half-past ten,' says I, 'and you are Andy Tucker. I've seen you work. Wasn't it you that put up the Great Cupid Combination package on the Southern States? Let's see, it was a Chilian diamond engagement ring, a wedding ring, a potato masher, a bottle of soothing syrup and Dorothy Vernon—all for fifty cents.'

"Andy was pleased to hear that I remembered him. He was a good street man; and he was more than that—he respected his profession, and he was satisfied with 300 per cent. profit. He had plenty of offers to go into the illegitimate drug and garden seed business; but he was never to be tempted off of the straight path.

"I wanted a partner, so Andy and me agreed to go out together. I told him about the situation in Fisher Hill and how finances was low on account of the local mixture of politics and jalap. Andy had just got in on the train that morning. He was pretty low himself, and was going to canvass the town for a few dollars to build a new battleship by popular subscription at Eureka Springs. So we went out and sat on the porch and talked it over.

"The next morning at eleven o'clock when I was sitting there alone, an Uncle Tom shuffles into the hotel and asked for the doctor to come and see Judge Banks, who, it seems, was the mayor and a mighty sick man.

"'I'm no doctor,' says I. 'Why don't you go and get the doctor?'

"'Boss,' says he, 'Doc Hoskins am done gone twenty miles in de country to see some sick persons. He's de only doctor in de town, and Massa Banks am powerful bad off. He sent me to ax you to please, suh, come.'

"'As man to man,' says I, 'I'll go and look him over.' So I put a bottle of Resurrection Bitters in my pocket and goes up on the hill to the Mayor's mansion, the finest house in town, with a mansard roof and two cast-iron dogs on the lawn.

"This Mayor Banks was in bed all but his whiskers and feet. He was making internal noises that would have had everybody in San Francisco hiking for the parks. A young man was standing by the bed holding a cup of water.

"'Doc,' says the Mayor, 'I'm awful sick.'

I'm about to die. Can't you do nothing for
me?'

"'Mr. Mayor,' says I, 'I'm not a regular
preordained disciple of S. Q. Lapius. I never
took a course in a medical college,' says I.
'I've just come as a fellow man to see if I
could be of assistance.'

"'I'm deeply obliged,' says he. 'Doc
Waugh-hoo, this is my nephew, Mr. Biddle.
He has tried to alleviate my distress, but
without success. Oh, Lordy! Ow-ow-ow!!'
he sings out.

"I nods at Mr. Biddle and sets down by the
bed and feels the Mayor's pulse. 'Let me
see your liver—your tongue, I mean,' says I.
Then I turns up the lids of his eyes and looks
close at the pupils of 'em.

"'How long have you been sick?' I asked.

"'I was taken down—ow-ouch—last night,'
says the Mayor. 'Gimme something for it,
doc, won't you?'

"'Mr. Fiddle,' says I, 'raise the window
shade a bit, will you?'

"'Biddle,' says the young man. 'Do you
feel like you could eat some ham and eggs,
Uncle James?'

"'Mr. Mayor,' says I, after laying my ear

to his right shoulder blade and listening, 'you've got a bad attack of super-inflammation of the right clavicle of the harpsichord!'

"'Good Lord!' says he, with a groan. 'Can't you rub something on it, or set it or anything?'

"I picks up my hat and starts for the door.

"'You ain't going, Doc?' says the Mayor with a howl. 'You ain't going away and leave me to die with this—superfluity of the clapboards, are you?'

"'Common humanity, Dr. Whoa-ha,' says Mr. Biddle, 'ought to prevent your deserting a fellow-human in distress.'

"'Dr. Waugh-hoo, when you get through plowing,' says I. And then I walks back to the bed and throws back my long hair.

"'Mr. Mayor,' says I, 'there is only one hope for you. Drugs will do you no good. But there is another power higher yet, although drugs are high enough,' says I.

"'And what is that?' says he.

"'Scientific demonstrations,' says I. 'The triumph of mind over sarsaparilla. The belief that there is no pain and sickness except what is produced when we ain't feeling well. Declare yourself in arrears. Demonstrate.'

"'What is this paraphernalia you speak of, Doc?' says the Mayor. 'You ain't a Socialist, are you?'

"'I am speaking,' says I, 'of the great doctrine of psychic financiering—of the enlightened school of long-distance, sub-conscientious treatment of fallacies and meningitis—of that wonderful indoor sport known as personal magnetism.'

"'Can you work it, Doc?' asks the Mayor.

"'I'm one of the Sole Sanhedrims and Ostensible Hooplas of the Inner Pulpit,' says I. 'The lame talk and the blind rubber whenever I make a pass at 'em. I am a medium, a coloratura hypnotist, and a spirituous control. It was only through me at the recent seances at Ann Arbor that the late president of the Vinegar Bitters Company could revisit the earth to communicate with his sister Jane. You see me peddling medicine on the streets,' says I, 'to the poor. I don't practice personal magnetism on them. I do not drag it in the dust,' says I, 'because they haven't got the dust.'

"'Will you treat my case?' asks the Mayor.

"'Listen,' says I. 'I've had a good deal of trouble with medical societies everywhere I've been. I don't practice medicine. But, to save your life, I'll give you the psychic treatment if you'll agree as mayor not to push the license question.'

"'Of course I will,' says he. 'And now get to work, Doc, for them pains are coming on again.'

"'My fee will be $250, cure guaranteed in two treatments,' says I.

"'All right,' says the Mayor. 'I'll pay it. I guess my life's worth that much.'

"I sat down by the bed and looked him straight in the eye.

"'Now,' says I, 'get your mind off the disease. You ain't sick. You haven't got a heart or a clavicle or a funny bone or brains or anything. You haven't got any pain. Declare error. Now you feel the pain that you didn't have leaving, don't you?'

"'I do feel some little better, Doc,' says the Mayor, 'darned if I don't. Now state a few lies about my not having this swelling in my left side, and I think I could be propped up and have some sausage and buckwheat cakes.'

"I made a few passes with my hands.

"'Now,' says I, 'the inflammation's gone. The right lobe of the perihelion has subsided.

You're getting sleepy. You can't hold your eyes open any longer. For the present the disease is checked. Now, you are asleep.'

"The Mayor shut his eyes slowly and began to snore.

"'You observe, Mr. Tiddle,' says I, 'the wonders of modern science.'

"'Biddle,' says he. 'When will you give uncle the rest of the treatment, Dr. Poohpooh?'

"'Waugh-hoo,' says I. 'I'll come back at eleven to-morrow. When he wakes up give him eight drops of turpentine and three pounds of steak. Good-morning.'

"The next morning I went back on time. 'Well, Mr. Riddle,' says I, when he opened the bedroom door, 'and how is uncle this morning?'

"'He seems much better,' says the young man.

"The Mayor's colour and pulse was fine. I gave him another treatment, and he said the last of the pain left him.

"'Now,' says I, 'you'd better stay in bed for a day or two, and you'll be all right. It's a good thing I happened to be in Fisher Hill, Mr. Mayor,' says I, 'for all the remedies in the cornucopia that the regular schools of medicine use couldn't have saved you. And now that error has flew and pain proved a perjurer, let's allude to a cheerfuller subject —say the fee of $250. No checks, please, I hate to write my name on the back of a check almost as bad as I do on the front.'

"'I've got the cash here,' says the Mayor, pulling a pocketbook from under his pillow.

"He counts out five fifty-dollar notes and holds 'em in his hand.

"'Bring the receipt,' he says to Biddle.

"I signed the receipt and the Mayor handed me the money. I put it in my inside pocket careful.

"'Now do your duty, officer,' says the Mayor, grinning much unlike a sick man.

"Mr. Biddle lays his hand on my arm.

"'You're under arrest, Dr. Waugh-hoo, alias Peters,' says he, 'for practising medicine without authority under the State law.'

"'Who are you?' I asks.

"'I'll tell you who he is,' says Mr. Mayor, sitting up in bed. 'He's a detective employed by the State Medical Society. He's been following you over five counties. He came to me yesterday and we fixed up this scheme to catch you. I guess you won't do any

more doctoring around these parts, Mr. Fakir.
What was it you said I had, Doc?' the Mayor
laughs, 'compound—well, it wasn't softening
of the brain, I guess, anyway.'

"'A detective,' says I.

"'Correct,' says Biddle. 'I'll have to turn
you over to the sheriff.'

"'Let's see you do it,' says I, and I grabs
Biddle by the throat and half throws him out
the window, but he pulls a gun and sticks
it under my chin, and I stand still. Then
he puts handcuffs on me, and takes the money
out of my pocket.

"'I witness,' says he, 'that they're the same
bills that you and I marked, Judge Banks.
I'll turn them over to the sheriff when we get
to his office, and he'll send you a receipt.
They'll have to be used as evidence in the
case.'

"'All right, Mr. Biddle,' says the mayor.
'And now, Doc Waugh-hoo,' he goes on, 'why
don't you demonstrate? Can't you pull the
cork out of your magnetism with your teeth
and hocus-pocus them handcuffs off?'

"'Come on, officer,' says I, dignified. 'I
may as well make the best of it.' And then I
turns to old Banks and rattles my chains.

"'Mr. Mayor,' says I, 'the time will come soon when you'll believe that personal magnetism is a success.   And you'll be sure that it succeeded in this case, too.'

"And I guess it did.

"When we got nearly to the gate, I says: 'We might meet somebody now, Andy.   I reckon you better take 'em off, and——' Hey? Why, of course it was Andy Tucker.   That was his scheme; and that's how we got the capital to go into business together."

VI

ONE DOLLAR'S WORTH

THE judge of the United States court of the district lying along the Rio Grande border found the following letter one morning in his mail:

JUDGE:

When you sent me up for four years you made a talk. Among other hard things, you called me a rattlesnake. Maybe I am one—anyhow, you hear me rattling now. One year after I got to the pen, my daughter died of—well, they said it was poverty and the disgrace together. You've got a daughter, Judge, and I'm going to make you know how it feels to lose one. And I'm going to bite that district attorney that spoke against me. I'm free now, and I guess I've turned to rattlesnake all right. I feel like one. I don't say much, but this is my rattle. Look out when I strike.

Yours respectfully,

RATTLESNAKE.

Judge Derwent threw the letter carelessly aside. It was nothing new to receive such epistles from desperate men whom he had been called upon to judge. He felt no alarm.

Later on he showed the letter to Littlefield, the young district attorney, for Littlefield's name was included in the threat, and the judge was punctilious in matters between himself and his fellowmen.

Littlefield honoured the rattle of the writer, as far as it concerned himself, with a smile of contempt; but he frowned a little over the reference to the Judge's daughter, for he and Nancy Derwent were to be married in the fall.

Littlefield went to the clerk of the court and looked over the records with him. They decided that the letter might have been sent by Mexico Sam, a half-breed border desperado who had been imprisoned for manslaughter four years before. Then official duties crowded the matter from his mind, and the rattle of the revengeful serpent was forgotten.

Court was in session at Brownsville. Most of the cases to be tried were charges of smuggling, counterfeiting, post-office robberies, and violations of Federal laws along the border. One case was that of a young Mexican, Rafael Ortiz, who had been rounded up by a clever deputy marshal in the act of passing a counterfeit silver dollar. He had been suspected of

many such deviations from rectitude, but this
was the first time that anything provable had
been fixed upon him.   Ortiz languished cozily
in jail, smoking brown cigarettes and waiting
for trial.   Kilpatrick, the deputy, brought the
counterfeit dollar and handed it to the district
attorney in his office in the court-house.   The
deputy and a reputable druggist were pre-
pared to swear that Ortiz paid for a bottle of
medicine with it.   The coin was a poor counterfeit, soft, dull-looking, and made principally
of lead.   It was the day before the morning
on which the docket would reach the case of
Ortiz, and the district attorney was preparing
himself for trial.

"Not much need of having in high-priced
experts to prove the coin's queer, is there,
Kil?" smiled Littlefield, as he thumped the
dollar down upon the table, where it fell with
no more ring than would have come from a
lump of putty.

"I guess the Greaser's as good as behind the
bars," said the deputy, easing up his holsters;
"You've got him dead.   If it had been just
one time, these Mexicans can't tell good
money from bad; but this little yaller rascal
belongs to a gang of counterfeiters, I know.

This is the first time I've been able to catch him doing the trick. He's got a girl down there in them Mexican jacals on the river bank. I seen her one day when I was watching him. She's as pretty as a red heifer in a flower bed."

Littlefield shoved the counterfeit dollar into his pocket, and slipped his memoranda of the case into an envelope. Just then a bright, winsome face, as frank and jolly as a boy's, appeared in the doorway, and in walked Nancy Derwent.

"Oh, Bob, didn't court adjourn at twelve to-day until to-morrow?" she asked of Littlefield.

"It did," said the district attorney, "and I'm very glad of it. I've got a lot of rulings to look up, and——"

"Now, that's just like you. I wonder you and father don't turn to law books or rulings or something! I want you to take me out plover-shooting this afternoon. Long Prairie is just alive with them. Don't say no, please! I want to try my new twelve-bore hammerless. I've sent to the livery stable to engage Fly and Bess for the buckboard; they stand fire so nicely. I was sure you would go."

They were to be married in the fall. The

glamour was at its height.   The plovers won
the day—or, rather, the afternoon—over the
calf-bound authorities.   Littlefield began to
put his papers away.

There was a knock at the door.   Kilpatrick
answered it.   A beautiful, dark-eyed girl
with a skin tinged with the faintest lemon
colour walked into the room.   A black shawl
was thrown over her head and wound once
around her neck.

She began to talk in Spanish, a voluble,
mournful stream of melancholy music.   Littlefield did not understand Spanish.   The
deputy did, and he translated her talk by portions, at intervals holding up his hand to check
the flow of her words.

"She came to see you, Mr. Littlefield.   Her
name's Joya Treviñas.   She wants to see you
about—well, she's mixed up with that Rafael
Ortiz.   She's his—she's his girl.   She says
he's innocent.   She says she made the money
and got him to pass it.   Don't you believe
her, Mr. Littlefield.   That's the way with
these Mexican girls; they'll lie, steal, or kill for
a fellow when they get stuck on him.   Never
trust a woman that's in love!"

"Mr. Kilpatrick!"

Nancy Derwent's indignant exclamation caused the deputy to flounder for a moment in attempting to explain that he had misquoted his own sentiments, and then he went on with the translation:

"She says she's willing to take his place in the jail if you'll let him out. She says she was down sick with the fever, and the doctor said she'd die if she didn't have medicine. That's why he passed the lead dollar on the drug store. She says it saved her life. This Rafael seems to be her honey, all right; there's a lot of stuff in her talk about love and such things that you don't want to hear."

It was an old story to the district attorney.

"Tell her," said he, "that I can do nothing. The case comes up in the morning, and he will have to make his fight before the court."

Nancy Derwent was not so hardened. She was looking with sympathetic interest at Joya Treviñas and at Littlefield alternately. The deputy repeated the district attorney's words to the girl. She spoke a sentence or two in a low voice, pulled her shawl closely about her face, and left the room.

"What did she say then?" asked the district attorney.

"Nothing special," said the deputy.   "She said: 'If the life of the one'—let's see how it went—'*Si la vida de ella á quien tu amas*—if the life of the girl you love is ever in danger, remember Rafael Ortiz.'"

Kilpatrick strolled out through the corridor in the direction of the marshal's office.

"Can't you do anything for them, Bob?" asked Nancy.   "It's such a little thing—just one counterfeit dollar—to ruin the happiness of two lives!   She was in danger of death, and he did it to save her.   Doesn't the law know the feeling of pity?"

"It hasn't a place in jurisprudence, Nan," said Littlefield, "especially *in re* the district attorney's duty.   I'll promise you that the prosecution will not be vindictive; but the man is as good as convicted when the case is called.   Witnesses will swear to his passing the bad dollar which I have in my pocket at this moment as 'Exhibit A.'   There are no Mexicans on the jury, and it will vote Mr. Greaser guilty without leaving the box."

The plover-shooting was fine that afternoon, and in the excitement of the sport the case of Rafael and the grief of Joya Treviñas

was forgotten. The district attorney and
Nancy Derwent drove out from the town three
miles along a smooth, grassy road, and then
struck across a rolling prairie toward a heavy
line of timber on Piedra Creek. Beyond this
creek lay Long Prairie, the favourite haunt
of the plover. As they were nearing the
creek they heard the galloping of a horse to
their right, and saw a man with black hair
and a swarthy face riding toward the woods
at a tangent, as if he had come up behind
them.

"I've seen that fellow somewhere," said
Littlefield, who had a memory for faces, "but
I can't exactly place him. Some ranchman,
I suppose, taking a short cut home."

They spent an hour on Long Prairie, shooting from the buckboard. Nancy Derwent,
an active, outdoor Western girl, was pleased
with her twelve-bore. She had bagged within
two brace of her companion's score.

They started homeward at a gentle trot.
When within a hundred yards of Piedra Creek
a man rode out of the timber directly toward
them.

"It looks like the man we saw coming over,"
remarked Miss Derwent.

As the distance between them lessened, the district attorney suddenly pulled up his team sharply, with his eyes fixed upon the advancing horseman. That individual had drawn a Winchester from its scabbard on his saddle and thrown it over his arm.

"Now I know you, Mexico Sam!" muttered Littlefield to himself. "It *was* you who shook your rattles in that gentle epistle."

Mexico Sam did not leave things long in doubt. He had a nice eye in all matters relating to firearms, so when he was within good rifle range, but outside of danger from No. 8 shot, he threw up his Winchester and opened fire upon the occupants of the buckboard.

The first shot cracked the back of the seat within the two-inch space between the shoulders of Littlefield and Miss Derwent. The next went through the dashboard and Littlefield's trouser leg.

The district attorney hustled Nancy out of the buckboard to the ground. She was a little pale, but asked no questions. She had the frontier instinct that accepts conditions in an emergency without superfluous argument. They kept their guns in hand, and

Littlefield hastily gathered some handfuls of cartridges from the pasteboard box on the seat and crowded them into his pockets.

"Keep behind the horses, Nan," he commanded. "That fellow is a ruffian I sent to prison once. He's trying to get even. He knows our shot won't hurt him at that distance."

"All right, Bob," said Nancy steadily. "I'm not afraid. But you come close, too. Whoa, Bess; stand still, now!"

She stroked Bess's mane. Littlefield stood with his gun ready, praying that the desperado would come within range.

But Mexico Sam was playing his vendetta along safe lines. He was a bird of different feather from the plover. His accurate eye drew an imaginary line of circumference around the area of danger from bird-shot, and upon this line he rode. His horse wheeled to the right, and as his victims rounded to the safe side of their equine breastwork he sent a ball through the district attorney's hat. Once he miscalculated in making a détour, and overstepped his margin. Littlefield's gun flashed, and Mexico Sam ducked his head to the harmless patter of the shot. A few of them stung his horse, which pranced promptly back to the safety line.

The desperado fired again. A little cry came from Nancy Derwent. Littlefield whirled, with blazing eyes, and saw the blood trickling down her cheek.

"I'm not hurt, Bob—only a splinter struck me. I think he hit one of the wheel-spokes."

"Lord!" groaned Littlefield. "If I only had a charge of buckshot!"

The ruffian got his horse still, and took careful aim. Fly gave a snort and fell in the harness, struck in the neck. Bess, now disabused of the idea that plover were being fired at, broke her traces and galloped wildly away. Mexico Sam sent a ball neatly through the fulness of Nancy Derwent's shooting jacket.

"Lie down—lie down!" snapped Littlefield. "Close to the horse—flat on the ground —so." He almost threw her upon the grass against the back of the recumbent Fly. Oddly enough, at that moment the words of the Mexican girl returned to his mind:

"If the life of the girl you love is ever in danger, remember Rafael Ortiz."

Littlefield uttered an exclamation.

"Open fire on him, Nan, across the horse's back! Fire as fast as you can! You can't hurt him, but keep him dodging shot for one minute while I try to work a little scheme."

Nancy gave a quick glance at Littlefield, and saw him take out his pocket-knife and open it. Then she turned her face to obey orders, keeping up a rapid fire at the enemy.

Mexico Sam waited patiently until this innocuous fusillade ceased. He had plenty of time, and he did not care to risk the chance of a bird-shot in his eye when it could be avoided by a little caution. He pulled his heavy Stetson low down over his face until the shots ceased. Then he drew a little nearer, and fired with careful aim at what he could see of his victims above the fallen horse.

Neither of them moved. He urged his horse a few steps nearer. He saw the district attorney rise to one knee and deliberately level his shotgun. He pulled his hat down and awaited the harmless rattle of the tiny pellets.

The shotgun blazed with a heavy report. Mexico Sam sighed, turned limp all over, and slowly fell from his horse—a dead rattlesnake.

At ten o'clock the next morning court opened, and the case of the United States *versus* Rafael Ortiz was called. The district attorney, with his arm in a sling, rose and addressed the court.

"May it please your honour," he said, "I desire to enter a *nolle pros.* in this case. Even though the defendant should be guilty, there is not sufficient evidence in the hands of the government to secure a conviction. The piece of counterfeit coin upon the identity of which the case was built is not now available as evidence. I ask, therefore, that the case be stricken off."

At the noon recess Kilpatrick strolled into the district attorney's office.

"I've just been down to take a squint at old Mexico Sam," said the deputy. "They've got him laid out. Old Mexico was a tough outfit, I reckon. The boys was wonderin' down there what you shot him with. Some said it must have been nails. I never see a gun carry anything to make holes like he had."

"I shot him," said the district attorney, "with Exhibit A of your counterfeiting case. Lucky thing for me—and somebody else—

that it was as bad money as it was! It sliced up into slugs very nicely. Say, Kil, can't you go down to the jacals and find where that Mexican girl lives? Miss Derwent wants to know."

VII

A CHAPARRAL CHRISTMAS GIFT

THE original cause of the trouble was about twenty years in growing.

At the end of that time it was worth it.

Had you lived anywhere within fifty miles of Sundown Ranch you would have heard of it. It possessed a quantity of jet-black hair, a pair of extremely frank, deep-brown eyes, and a laugh that rippled across the prairie like the sound of a hidden brook. The name of it was Rosita McMullen; and she was the daughter of old man McMullen of the Sundown Sheep Ranch.

There came riding on red roan steeds—or, to be more explicit, on a paint and a flea-bitten sorrel—two wooers. One was Madison Lane, and the other was the Frio Kid. But at that time they did not call him the Frio Kid, for he had not earned the honours of special nomenclature. His name was simply Johnny McRoy.

It must not be supposed that these two were
the sum of the agreeable Rosita's admirers.
The bronchos of a dozen others champed their
bits at the long hitching rack of the Sundown
Ranch.   Many were the sheep-eyes that were
cast in those savannas that did not belong to
the flocks of Dan McMullen.   But of all the
cavaliers, Madison Lane and Johnny McRoy
galloped far ahead, wherefore they are to be
chronicled.

Madison Lane, a young cattleman from the
Nueces country, won the race.   He and Rosita
were married one Christmas day.   Armed,
hilarious, vociferous, magnanimous, the cow-
men and the sheepmen, laying aside their
hereditary hatred, joined forces to celebrate
the occasion.

Sundown Ranch was sonorous with the
cracking of jokes and sixshooters, the shine
of buckles and bright eyes, the outspoken
congratulations of the herders of kine.

But while the wedding feast was at its
liveliest there descended upon it Johnny
McRoy, bitten by jealousy, like one possessed.

"I'll give you a Christmas present," he
yelled, shrilly, at the door, with his .45 in

his hand. Even then he had some reputation as an offhand shot.

His first bullet cut a neat underbit in Madison Lane's right ear. The barrel of his gun moved an inch. The next shot would have been the bride's had not Carson, a sheepman, possessed a mind with triggers somewhat well oiled and in repair. The guns of the wedding party had been hung, in their belts, upon nails in the wall when they sat at table, as a concession to good taste. But Carson, with great promptness, hurled his plate of roast venison and frijoles at McRoy, spoiling his aim. The second bullet, then, only shattered the white petals of a Spanish dagger flower suspended two feet above Rosita's head.

The guests spurned their chairs and jumped for their weapons. It was considered an improper act to shoot the bride and groom at a wedding. In about six seconds there were twenty or so bullets due to be whizzing in the direction of Mr. McRoy.

"I'll shoot better next time," yelled Johnny; "and there'll be a next time." He backed rapidly out the door.

Carson, the sheepman, spurred on to attempt further exploits by the success of his plate-throwing, was first to reach the door. McRoy's bullet from the darkness laid him low.

The cattlemen then swept out upon him, calling for vengeance, for, while the slaughter of a sheepman has not always lacked con- donement, it was a decided misdemeanour in this instance. Carson was innocent; he was no accomplice at the matrimonial proceedings; nor had any one heard him quote the line "Christmas comes but once a year" to the guests.

But the sortie failed in its vengeance. McRoy was on his horse and away, shouting back curses and threats as he galloped into the concealing chaparral.

That night was the birthnight of the Frio Kid. He became the "bad man" of that por- tion of the State. The rejection of his suit by Miss McMullen turned him to a dangerous man. When officers went after him for the shooting of Carson, he killed two of them, and entered upon the life of an outlaw. He be- came a marvellous shot with either hand. He would turn up in towns and settlements, raise a quarrel at the slightest opportunity, pick off his man, and laugh at the officers of the

law. He was so cool, so deadly, so rapid, so
inhumanly blood-thirsty that none but faint
attempts were ever made to capture him.
When he was at last shot and killed by a little
one-armed Mexican who was nearly dead himself from fright, the Frio Kid had the deaths
of eighteen men on his head. About half of
these were killed in fair duels depending upon
the quickness of the draw. The other half
were men whom he assassinated from absolute
wantonness and cruelty.

Many tales are told along the border of his
impudent courage and daring. But he was
not one of the breed of desperadoes who have
seasons of generosity and even of softness.
They say he never had mercy on the object of
his anger. Yet at this and every Christmas-
tide it is well to give each one credit, if it can
be done, for whatever speck of good he may
have possessed. If the Frio Kid ever did a
kindly act or felt a throb of generosity in his
heart it was once at such a time and season,
and this is the way it happened.

One who has been crossed in love should
never breathe the odour from the blossoms of
the ratama tree. It stirs the memory to a
dangerous degree.

One December in the Frio country there was a ratama tree in full bloom, for the winter had been as warm as springtime. That way rode the Frio Kid and his satellite and co-murderer, Mexican Frank. The kid reined in his mustang, and sat in his saddle, thoughtful and grim, with dangerously narrowing eyes. The rich, sweet scent touched him somewhere beneath his ice and iron.

"I don't know what I've been thinking about, Mex," he remarked in his usual mild drawl, "to have forgot all about a Christmas present I got to give. I'm going to ride over to-morrow night and shoot Madison Lane in his own house. He got my girl—Rosita would have had me if he hadn't cut into the game. I wonder why I happened to overlook it up to now?"

"Ah, shucks, Kid," said Mexican, "don't talk foolishness. You know you can't get within a mile of Mad Lane's house to-morrow night. I see old man Allen day before yesterday, and he says Mad is going to have Christmas doings at his house. You remember how you shot up the festivities when Mad was married, and about the threats you made? Don't you suppose Mad Lane'll kind of keep

his eye open for a certain Mr. Kid? You
plumb make me tired, Kid, with such remarks."

"I'm going," repeated the Frio Kid, without heat, "to go to Madison Lane's Christmas
doings, and kill him. I ought to have done it
a long time ago. Why, Mex, just two weeks
ago I dreamed me and Rosita was married
instead of her and him; and we was living in a
house, and I could see her smiling at me, and
—oh! h——l, Mex, he got her; and I'll get
him—yes, sir, on Christmas Eve he got her,
and then's when I'll get him."

"There's other ways of committing suicide,"
advised Mexican. "Why don't you go and
surrender to the sheriff?"

"I'll get him," said the Kid.

Christmas Eve fell as balmy as April.
Perhaps there was a hint of far-away frostiness
in the air, but it tingled like seltzer, perfumed
faintly with late prairie blossoms and the mesquite grass.

When night came the five or six rooms of the
ranch-house were brightly lit. In one room
was a Christmas tree, for the Lanes had a
boy of three, and a dozen or more guests were
expected from the nearer ranches.

At nightfall Madison Lane called aside Jim Belcher and three other cowboys employed on his ranch.

"Now, boys," said Lane, "keep your eyes open. Walk around the house and watch the road well. All of you know the 'Frio Kid,' as they call him now, and if you see him, open fire on him without asking any questions. I'm not afraid of his coming around, but Rosita is. She's been afraid he'd come in on us every Christmas since we were married."

The guests had arrived in buckboards and on horseback, and were making themselves comfortable inside.

The evening went along pleasantly. The guests enjoyed and praised Rosita's excellent supper, and afterward the men scattered in groups about the rooms or on the broad "gallery," smoking and chatting.

The Christmas tree, of course, delighted the youngsters, and above all were they pleased when Santa Claus himself in magnificent white beard and furs appeared and began to distribute the toys.

"It's my papa," announced Billy Sampson, aged six. "I've seen him wear 'em before."

Berkly, a sheepman, an old friend of Lane,

'stopped Rosita as she was passing by him on the gallery, where he was sitting smoking.

"Well, Mrs. Lane," said he, "I suppose by this Christmas you've gotten over being afraid of that fellow McRoy, haven't you? Madison and I have talked about it, you know."

"Very nearly," said Rosita, smiling, "but I am still nervous sometimes. I shall never forget that awful time when he came so near to killing us."

"He's the most cold-hearted villain in the world," said Berkly. "The citizens all along the border ought to turn out and hunt him down like a wolf."

"He has committed awful crimes," said Rosita, "but—I—don't—know. I think there is a spot of good somewhere in everybody. He was not always bad—that I know."

Rosita turned into the hallway between the rooms. Santa Claus, in muffling whiskers and furs, was just coming through.

"I heard what you said through the window, Mrs. Lane," he said. "I was just going down in my pocket for a Christmas present for your husband. But I've left one for you, instead. It's in the room to your right."

"Oh, thank you, kind Santa Claus," said Rosita brightly.

Rosita went into the room, while Santa Claus stepped into the cooler air of the yard.

She found no one in the room but Madison.

"Where is my present that Santa said he left for me in here?" she asked.

"Haven't seen anything in the way of a present," said her husband, laughing, "unless he could have meant me."

The next day Gabriel Radd, the foreman of the X O Ranch, dropped into the post-office at Loma Alta.

"Well, the Frio Kid's got his dose of lead at last," he remarked to the postmaster.

"That so? How'd it happen?"

"One of old Sanchez's Mexican sheep herders did it!—think of it! the Frio Kid killed by a sheep herder! The Greaser saw him riding along past his camp about twelve o'clock last night, and was so skeered that he up with a Winchester and let him have it. Funniest part of it was that the Kid was dressed all up with white Angora-skin whiskers and a regular Santy Claus rig-out from head to foot. Think of the Frio Kid playing Santy!"

VIII

THE ROADS WE TAKE

TWENTY miles west of Tucson the "Sunset Express" stopped at a tank to take on water. Besides the aqueous addition the engine of that famous flyer acquired some other things that were not good for it.

While the fireman was lowering the feeding hose, Bob Tidball, "Shark" Dodson, and a quarter-bred Creek Indian called John Big Dog climbed on the engine and showed the engineer three round orifices in pieces of ordnance that they carried. These orifices so impressed the engineer with their possibilities that he raised both hands in a gesture such as accompanies the ejaculation "Do tell!"

At the crisp command of Shark Dodson, who was leader of the attacking force, the engineer descended to the ground and uncoupled the engine and tender. Then John Big Dog, perched upon the coal, sportively

held two guns upon the engine driver and the
fireman, and suggested that they run the
engine fifty yards away and there await further
orders.

Shark Dodson and Bob Tidball, scorning
to put such low-grade ore as the passengers
through the mill, struck out for the rich pocket
of the express car.   They found the messenger
serene in the belief that the "Sunset Express"
was taking on nothing more stimulating and
dangerous than aqua pura.   While Bob was
knocking this idea out of his head with the
butt-end of his six-shooter Shark Dodson
was already dosing the express-car safe with
dynamite.

The safe exploded to the tune of $30,000,
all gold and currency.   The passengers thrust
their heads casually out of the windows to
look for the thunder-cloud.   The conductor
jerked at the bell-rope, which sagged down,
loose and unresisting, at his tug.   Shark Dodson and Bob Tidball, with their booty in a
stout canvas bag, tumbled out of the express
car and ran awkwardly in their high-heeled
boots to the engine.

The engineer, sullenly angry but wise, ran
the engine, according to orders, rapidly away

from the inert train.   But before this was accomplished the express messenger, recovered
from Bob Tidball's persuader to neutrality,
jumped out of his car with a Winchester rifle
and took a trick in the game. Mr. John
Big Dog, sitting on the coal tender, unwittingly
made a wrong lead by giving an imitation of
a target, and the messenger trumped him.
With a ball exactly between his shoulder-
blades the Creek chevalier of industry rolled
off to the ground, thus increasing the share of
his comrades in the loot by one-sixth each.

Two miles from the tank the engineer was
ordered to stop.

The robbers waved a defiant adieu and
plunged down the steep slope into the thick
woods that lined the track. Five minutes of
crashing through a thicket of chaparral
brought them to open woods, where three
horses were tied to low-hanging branches.
One was waiting for John Big Dog, who
would never ride by night or day again.
This animal the robbers divested of saddle
and bridle and set free. They mounted the
other two with the bag across one pommel,
and rode fast and with discretion through
the forest and up a primeval, lonely gorge.

Here the animal that bore Bob Tidball slipped
on a mossy boulder and broke a foreleg. They
shot him through the head at once and sat
down to hold a council of flight. Made secure for the present by the tortuous trail they
had travelled, the question of time was no
longer so big. Many miles and hours lay
between them and the spryest posse that could
follow. Shark Dodson's horse, with trailing
rope and dropped bridle, panted and cropped
thankfully of the grass along the stream in
the gorge. Bob Tidball opened the sack,
drew out double handfuls of the neat packages
of currency and the one sack of gold and
chuckled with the glee of a child.

"Say, you old double-decked pirate," he
called joyfully to Dodson, "you said we could
do it—you got a head for financing that
knocks the horns off of anything in Arizona."

"What are we going to do about a hoss
for you, Bob? We ain't got long to wait
here. They'll be on our trail before daylight
in the mornin'."

"Oh, I guess that cayuse of yourn'll carry
double for a while," answered the sanguine
Bob. "We'll annex the first animal we come
across. By jingoes, we made a haul, didn't

we? Accordin' to the marks on this money there's $30,000—$15,000 apiece!"

"It's short of what I expected," said Shark Dodson, kicking softly at the packages with the toe of his boot. And then he looked pensively at the wet sides of his tired horse.

"Old Bolivar's mighty nigh played out," he said slowly. "I wish that sorrel of yours hadn't got hurt."

"So do I," said Bob, heartily, "but it can't be helped. Bolivar's got plenty of bottom —he'll get us both far enough to get fresh mounts. Dang it, Shark, I can't help thinkin' how funny it is that an Easterner like you can come out here and give us Western fellows cards and spades in the desperado business. What part of the East was you from, anyway?"

"New York State," said Shark Dodson, sitting down on a boulder and chewing a twig. "I was born on a farm in Ulster County. I ran away from home when I was seventeen. It was an accident my comin' West. I was walkin' along the road with my clothes in a bundle, makin' for New York City. I had an idea of goin' there and makin' lots of money. I always felt like I could do it. I came to a

place one evenin' where the road forked and
I didn't know which fork to take. I studied
about it for half an hour, and then I took
the left hand. That night I run into the camp
of a Wild West show that was travellin'
among the little towns, and I went West with
it. I've often wondered if I wouldn't have
turned out different if I'd took the other road."

"Oh, I reckon you'd have ended up about
the same," said Bob Tidball, cheerfully philo-
sophical. "It ain't the roads we take; it's
what's inside of us that makes us turn out
the way we do."

Shark Dodson got up and leaned against a
tree.

"I'd a good deal rather that sorrel of yourn
hadn't hurt himself, Bob," he said again, almost pathetically.

"Same here," agreed Bob; "he was sure a
first-rate kind of a crowbait. But Bolivar,
he'll pull us through all right. Reckon we'd
better be movin' on, hadn't we, Shark? I'll
bag this boodle ag'in and we'll hit the trail
for higher timber."

Bob Tidball replaced the spoil in the bag
and tied the mouth of it tightly with a cord.
When he looked up the most prominent ob-

ject that he saw was the muzzle of Shark
Dodson's .45 held upon him without a waver.

"Stop your funnin'," said Bob, with a grin.
"We got to be hittin' the breeze."

"Set still," said Shark. "You ain't goin'
to hit no breeze, Bob. I hate to tell you,
but there ain't any chance for but one of us.
Bolivar, he's plenty tired, and he can't carry
double."

"We been pards, me and you, Shark
Dodson, for three year," Bob said quietly.
"We've risked our lives together time and
again. I've always give you a square deal,
and I thought you was a man. I've heard
some queer stories about you shootin' one or
two men in a peculiar way, but I never believed 'em. Now if you're just havin' a little
fun with me, Shark, put your gun up, and
we'll get on Bolivar and vamose. If you
mean to shoot—shoot, you blackhearted son
of a tarantula!"

Shark Dodson's face bore a deeply sorrow-
ful look.

"You don't know how bad I feel," he
sighed, "about that sorrel of yourn breakin'
his leg, Bob."

The expression on Dodson's face changed in

an instant to one of cold ferocity mingled with inexorable cupidity. The soul of the man showed itself for a moment like an evil face in the window of a reputable house.

Truly Bob Tidball was never to "hit the breeze" again. The deadly .45 of the false friend cracked and filled the gorge with a roar that the walls hurled back with indignant echoes. And Bolivar, unconscious accomplice, swiftly bore away the last of the holders-up of the "Sunset Express," not put to the stress of "carrying double."

But as "Shark" Dodson galloped away the woods seemed to fade from his view; the revolver in his right hand turned to the curved arm of a mahogany chair; his saddle was strangely upholstered, and he opened his eyes and saw his feet, not in stirrups, but resting quietly on the edge of a quartered-oak desk.

I am telling you that Dodson, of the firm of Dodson & Decker, Wall Street brokers, opened his eyes. Peabody, the confidential clerk, was standing by his chair, hesitating to speak. There was a confused hum of wheels below, and the sedative buzz of an electric fan.

"Ahem! Peabody," said Dodson, blinking. "I must have fallen asleep. I had a most remarkable dream. What is it, Peabody?"

"Mr. Williams, sir, of Tracy & Williams, is outside. He has come to settle his deal in X. Y. Z. The market caught him short, sir, if you remember."

"Yes, I remember. What is X. Y. Z. quoted at to-day, Peabody?"

"One eighty-five, sir."

"Then that's his price."

"Excuse me," said Peabody, rather nervously, "for speaking of it, but I've been talking to Williams. He's an old friend of yours, Mr. Dodson, and you practically have a corner in X. Y. Z. I thought you might—that is, I thought you might not remember that he sold you the stock at 98. If he settles at the market price it will take every cent he has in the world and his home, too, to deliver the shares."

The expression on Dodson's face changed in an instant to one of cold ferocity mingled with inexorable cupidity. The soul of the man showed itself for a moment like an evil face in the window of a reputable house.

"He will settle at one eighty-five," said Dodson. "Bolivar cannot carry double."

IX

NEW YORK BY CAMP FIRE LIGHT

AWAY out in the Creek Nation we learned things about New York.

We were on a hunting trip, and were camped one night on the bank of a little stream. Bud Kingsbury was our skilled hunter and guide, and it was from his lips that we had explanations of Manhattan and the queer folks that inhabit it. Bud had once spent a month in the metropolis, and a week or two at other times, and he was pleased to discourse to us of what he had seen.

Fifty yards away from our camp was pitched the teepee of a wandering family of Indians that had come up and settled there for the night. An old, old Indian woman was trying to build a fire under an iron pot hung upon three sticks.

Bud went over to her assistance, and soon had her fire going. When he came back we complimented him playfully upon his gallantry.

"Oh," said Bud, "don't mention it. It's a way I have. Whenever I see a lady trying to cook things in a pot and having trouble I always go to the rescue. I done the same thing once in a high-toned house in New York City. Heap big society teepee on Fifth Avenue. That Injun lady kind of recalled it to my mind. Yes, I endeavours to be polite and help the ladies out."

The camp demanded the particulars.

"I was manager of the Triangle B Ranch in the Panhandle," said Bud. "It was owned at that time by old man Sterling, of New York. He wanted to sell out, and he wrote for me to come on to New York and explain the ranch to the syndicate that wanted to buy. So I sends to Fort Worth and has a forty-dollar suit of clothes made, and hits the trail for the big village.

"Well, when I got there, old man Sterling and his outfit certainly laid themselves out to be agreeable. We had business and pleasure so mixed up that you couldn't tell whether it was a treat or a trade half the time. We had trolley rides, and cigars, and theatre round-ups, and rubber parties."

"Rubber parties?" said a listener inquiringly.

"Sure," said Bud. "Didn't you never attend 'em? You walk around and try to look at the tops of the skyscrapers. Well, we sold the ranch, and old man Sterling asks me 'round to his house to take grub on the night before I started back. It wasn't any high-collared affair—just me and the old man and his wife and daughter. But they was a fine-haired outfit all right, and the lilies of the field wasn't in it. They made my Fort Worth clothes carpenter look like a dealer in horse blankets and gee strings. And then the table was all pompous with flowers, and there was a whole kit of tools laid out beside everybody's plate. You'd have thought you was fixed out to burglarize a restaurant before you could get your grub. But I'd been in New York over a week then, and I was getting on to stylish ways. I kind of trailed behind and watched the others use the hardware supplies, and then I tackled the chuck with the same weapons. It ain't much trouble to travel with the high-flyers after you find out their gait. I got along fine. I was feeling cool and agreeable, and pretty soon I was talking away fluent as you please, all about the ranch and the West, and telling 'em how the

Indians eat grasshopper stew and snakes, and you never saw people so interested.

"But the real joy of that feast was that Miss Sterling. Just a little trick she was, not bigger than two bits worth of chewing plug; but she had a way about her that seemed to say she was the people, and you believed it. And yet, she never put on any airs, and she smiled at me the same as if I was a millionaire while I was telling about a Creek dog feast and listened like it was news from home.

"By and by, after we had eat oysters and some watery soup and truck that never was in my repertory, a Methodist preacher brings in a kind of camp stove arrangement, all silver, on long legs, with a lamp under it.

"Miss Sterling lights up and begins to do some cooking right on the supper table. I wondered why old man Sterling didn't hire a cook, with all the money he had. Pretty soon she dished out some cheesy tasting truck that she said was rabbit, but I swear there had never been a Molly cotton tail in a mile of it.

"The last thing on the programme was lemonade. It was brought around in little flat glass bowls and set by your plate. I was

pretty thirsty, and I picked up mine and took
a big swig of it.   Right there was where the
little lady had made a mistake.   She had put
in the lemon all right, but she'd forgot the
sugar.   The best housekeepers slip up sometimes.   I thought maybe Miss Sterling was
just learning to keep house and cook—that
rabbit would surely make you think so—and
I says to myself, 'Little lady, sugar or no
sugar I'll stand by you,' and I raises up my
bowl again and drinks the last drop of the
lemonade.   And then all the balance of 'em
picks up their bowls and does the same.   And
then I gives Miss Sterling the laugh proper,
just to carry it off like a joke, so she wouldn't
feel bad about the mistake.

"After we all went into the sitting room she
sat down and talked to me quite awhile.

"'It was so kind of you, Mr. Kingsbury,'
says she, 'to bring my blunder off so nicely.
It was so stupid of me to forget the sugar.'

"'Never you mind,' says I, 'some lucky
man will throw his rope over a mighty elegant
little housekeeper some day, not far from
here.

"'If you mean me, Mr. Kingsbury,' says she,
laughing out loud, 'I hope he will be as

lenient with my poor housekeeping as you have been.'

"'Don't mention it,' says I. 'Anything to oblige the ladies.'"

Bud ceased his reminiscences. And then some one asked him what he considered the most striking and prominent trait of New Yorkers.

"The most visible and peculiar trait of New York folks," answered Bud, "is New York. Most of 'em has New York on the brain. They have heard of other places, such as Waco, and Paris, and Hot Springs, and London; but they don't believe in 'em. They think that town is all Merino. Now to show you how much they care for their village I'll tell you about one of 'em that strayed out as far as the Triangle B while I was working there.

"This New Yorker come out there looking for a job on the ranch. He said he was a good horseback rider, and there was pieces of tanbark hanging on his clothes yet from his riding school.

"Well, for a while they put him to keeping books in the ranch store, for he was a devil at figures. But he got tired of that, and

asked for something more in the line of ac-
tivity.   The boys on the ranch liked him all
right, but he made us tired shouting New
York all the time.   Every night he'd tell us
about East River and J. P. Morgan and the
Eden Musee and Hetty Green and Central
Park till we used to throw tin plates and
branding irons at him.

"One day this chap gets on a pitching pony,
and the pony kind of sidled up his back and
went to eating grass while the New Yorker
was coming down.

"He come down on his head on a chunk of
mesquite wood, and he didn't show any designs toward getting up again.   We laid him
out in a tent, and he begun to look pretty
dead.   So Gideon Pease saddles up and
burns the wind for old Doc Sleeper's residence
in Dogtown, thirty miles away.

"The doctor comes over and he investigates
the patient.

"'Boys,' says he, 'you might as well go to
playing seven-up for his saddle and clothes,
for his head's fractured and if he lives ten
minutes it will be a remarkable case of longe-
vity.'

"Of course we didn't gamble for the poor

rooster's saddle—that was one of Doc's jokes. But we stood around feeling solemn, and all of us forgive him for having talked us to death about New York.

"I never saw anybody about to hand in his checks act more peaceful than this fellow. His eyes were fixed 'way up in the air, and he was using rambling words to himself all about sweet music and beautiful streets and white-robed forms, and he was smiling like dying was a pleasure.

"'He's about gone now,' said Doc. 'Whenever they begin to think they see heaven it's all off.'

"Blamed if that New York man didn't sit right up when he heard the Doc say that.

"'Say,' says he, kind of disappointed, 'was that heaven? Confound it all, I thought it was Broadway. Some of you fellows get my clothes. I'm going to get up.'

"And I'll be blamed," concluded Bud, "if he wasn't on the train with a ticket for New York in his pocket four days afterward!"

X

THE ADVENTURES OF SHAMROCK JOLNES

I AM so fortunate as to count Shamrock Jolnes, the great New York detective, among my muster of friends. Jolnes is what is called the "inside man" of the city detective force. He is an expert in the use of the typewriter, and it is his duty, whenever there is a "murder mystery" to be solved, to sit at a desk telephone at Headquarters and take down the messages of "cranks" who 'phone in their confessions to having committed the crime.

But on certain "off" days when confessions are coming in slowly and three or four newspapers have run to earth as many different guilty persons, Jolnes will knock about the town with me, exhibiting, to my great delight and instruction, his marvellous powers of observation and deduction.

The other day I dropped in at Headquarters and found the great detective gazing thoughtfully at a string that was tied tightly around his little finger.

"Good morning, Whatsup," he said, without turning his head. "I'm glad to notice that you've had your house fitted up with electric lights at last."

"Will you please tell me," I said, in surprise, "how you knew that? I am sure that I never mentioned the fact to any one, and the wiring was a rush order not completed until this morning."

"Nothing easier," said Jolnes genially. "As you came in I caught the odour of the cigar you are smoking. I know an expensive cigar; and I know that not more than three men in New York can afford to smoke cigars and pay gas bills, too, at the present time. That was an easy one. But I am working just now on a little problem of my own."

"Why have you that string on your finger?" I asked.

"That's the problem," said Jolnes. "My wife tied that on this morning to remind me of something I was to send up to the house. Sit down, Whatsup, and excuse me for a few moments."

The distinguished detective went to a wall

telephone, and stood with the receiver to his ear for probably ten minutes.

"Were you listening to a confession?" I asked, when he had returned to his chair.

"Perhaps," said Jolnes, with a smile, "it might be called something of the sort. To be frank with you, Whatsup, I've cut out the dope. I've been increasing the quantity for so long that morphine doesn't have much effect on me any more. I've got to have something more powerful. That telephone I just went to is connected with a room in the Waldorf where there's an author's reading in progress. Now, to get at the solution of this string."

After five minutes of silent pondering Jolnes looked at me, with a smile, and nodded his head.

"Wonderful man!" I exclaimed; "already?"

"It is quite simple," he said, holding up his finger. "You see that knot? That is to prevent my forgetting. It is, therefore, a forget-me-knot. A forget-me-not is a flower. It was a sack of flour that I was to send home!"

"Beautiful!" I could not help crying out in admiration.

"Suppose we go out for a ramble," suggested Jolnes. "There is only one case of importance on hand just now. Old man McCarty, one hundred and four years old, died from eating too many bananas. The evidence points so strongly to the Mafia that the police have surrounded the Second Avenue Katzenjammer Gambrinus Club No. 2, and the capture of the assassin is only the matter of a few hours. The detective force has not yet been called on for assistance."

Jolnes and I went out and up the street toward the corner, where we were to catch a surface car.

Halfway up the block we met Rheingelder, an acquaintance of ours, who held a City Hall position.

"Good morning, Rheingelder," said Jolnes, halting.

"Nice breakfast that was you had this morning."

Always on the lookout for the detective's remarkable feats of deduction, I saw Jolnes's eye flash for an instant upon a long yellow splash on the shirt bosom and a smaller one upon the chin of Rheingelder—both undoubtedly made by the yolk of an egg.

"Oh, dot is some of your detectiveness," said Rheingelder, shaking all over with a smile. "Vell, I pet you trinks and cigars all round dot you cannot tell vot I haf eaten for breakfast."

"Done," said Jolnes. "Sausage, pumpernickel, and coffee."

Rheingelder admitted the correctness of the surmise and paid the bet. When we had proceeded on our way I said to Jolnes:

"I thought you looked at the egg spilled on his chin and shirt front."

"I did," said Jolnes. "That is where I began my deduction. Rheingelder is a very economical, saving man. Yesterday eggs dropped in the market to twenty-eight cents per dozen. To-day they are quoted at forty-two. Rheingelder ate eggs yesterday, and to-day he went back to his usual fare. A little thing like this isn't anything, Whatsup; it belongs to the primary arithmetic class."

When we boarded the street car we found the seats all occupied—principally by ladies. Jolnes and I stood on the rear platform.

About the middle of the car there sat an elderly man with a short, gray beard, who looked to be the typical, well-dressed New Yorker. At successive corners other ladies climbed aboard, and soon three or four of them were standing over the man, clinging to straps and glaring meaningly at the man who occupied the coveted seat. But he resolutely retained his place.

"We New Yorkers," I remarked to Jolnes, "have about lost our manners, as far as the exercise of them in public goes."

"Perhaps so," said Jolnes, lightly; "but the man you evidently refer to happens to be a very chivalrous and courteous gentleman from Old Virginia. He is spending a few days in New York with his wife and two daughters, and he leaves for the South to-night."

"You know him, then?" I said, in amazement.

"I never saw him before we stepped on the car," declared the detective smilingly.

"By the gold tooth of the Witch of Endor!" I cried, "if you can construe all that from his appearance you are dealing in nothing else than black art."

"The habit of observation—nothing more," said Jolnes. "If the old gentleman gets off the car before we do, I think I can demonstrate to you the accuracy of my deduction."

Three blocks farther along the gentleman rose to leave the car. Jolnes addressed him at the door:

"Pardon me, sir, but are you not Colonel Hunter, of Norfolk, Virginia?"

"No, suh," was the extremely courteous answer. "My name, suh, is Ellison—Major Winfield R. Ellison, from Fairfax County, in the same state. I know a good many people, suh, in Norfolk—the Goodriches, the Tollivers, and the Crabtrees, suh, but I never had the pleasure of meeting yo' friend, Colonel Hunter. I am happy to say, suh, that I am going back to Virginia to-night, after having spent a week in yo' city with my wife and three daughters. I shall be in Norfolk in about ten days, and if you will give me yo' name, suh, I will take pleasure in looking up Colonel Hunter and telling him that you inquired after him, suh."

"Thank you," said Jolnes; "tell him that Reynolds sent his regards, if you will be so kind."

I glanced at the great New York detective and saw that a look of intense chagrin had come upon his clear-cut features. Failure in the slightest point always galled Shamrock Jolnes.

"Did you say your *three* daughters?" he asked of the Virginia gentleman.

"Yes, suh, my three daughters, all as fine girls as there are in Fairfax County," was the answer.

With that Major Ellison stopped the car and began to descend the step.

Shamrock Jolnes clutched his arm.

"One moment, sir," he begged, in an urbane voice in which I alone detected the anxiety— "am I not right in believing that one of the young ladies is an *adopted* daughter?"

"You are, suh," admitted the major, from the ground, "but how the devil you knew it, suh, is mo' than I can tell."

"And mo' than I can tell, too," I said, as the car went on.

Jolnes was restored to his calm, observant serenity by having wrested victory from his apparent failure; so after we got off the car he invited me into a café, promising to reveal the process of his latest wonderful feat.

"In the first place," he began after we were comfortably seated, "I knew the gentleman was no New Yorker because he was flushed

and uneasy and restless on account of the
ladies that were standing, although he did
not rise and give them his seat. I decided
from his appearance that he was a Southerner
rather than a Westerner.

"Next I began to figure out his reason for
not relinquishing his seat to a lady when he
evidently felt strongly, but not overpower-
ingly, impelled to do so. I very quickly decided upon that. I noticed that one of his
eyes had received a severe jab in one corner,
which was red and inflamed, and that all
over his face were tiny round marks about
the size of the end of an uncut lead pencil.
Also upon both of his patent leather shoes
were a number of deep imprints shaped like
ovals cut off square at one end.

"Now, there is only one district in New York
City where a man is bound to receive scars
and wounds and indentations of that sort—
and that is along the sidewalks of Twenty-
third Street and a portion of Sixth Avenue
south of there. I knew from the imprints of
trampling French heels on his feet and the
marks of countless jabs in the face from um-
brellas and parasols carried by women in the
shopping district that he had been in conflict

with the amazonian troops. And as he was a man of intelligent appearance, I knew he would not have braved such dangers unless he had been dragged thither by his own women folk. Therefore, when he got on the car his anger at the treatment he had received was sufficient to make him keep his seat in spite of his traditions of Southern chivalry."

"That is all very well," I said, "but why did you insist upon daughters—and especially two daughters? Why couldn't a wife alone have taken him shopping?"

"There had to be daughters," said Jolnes calmly. "If he had only a wife, and she near his own age, he could have bluffed her into going alone. If he had a young wife she would prefer to go alone. So there you are."

"I'll admit that," I said; "but, now, why two daughters? And how, in the name of all the prophets, did you guess that one was adopted when he told you he had three?"

"Don't say guess," said Jolnes, with a touch of pride in his air; "there is no such word in the lexicon of ratiocination. In Major Ellison's buttonhole there was a carnation and a rosebud backed by a geranium leaf. No woman ever combined a carnation and a rosebud into a boutonnière. Close your eyes, Whatsup, and give the logic of your imagination a chance. Cannot you see the lovely Adele fastening the carnation to the lapel so that papa may be gay upon the street? And then the romping Edith May dancing up with sisterly jealousy to add her rosebud to the adornment?"

"And then," I cried, beginning to feel enthusiasm, "when he declared that he had three daughters"——

"I could see," said Jolnes, "one in the background who added no flower; and I knew that she must be——"

"Adopted!" I broke in. "I give you every credit; but how did you know he was leaving for the South to-night?"

"In his breast pocket," said the great detective, "something large and oval made a protuberance. Good liquor is scarce on trains, and it is a long journey from New York to Fairfax County."

"Again, I must bow to you," I said. "And tell me this, so that my last shred of doubt will be cleared away; why did you decide that he was from Virginia?"

"It was very faint, I admit," answered Shamrock Jolnes, "but no trained observer could have failed to detect the odour of mint in the car."

XI

THE SLEUTHS

In the Big City a man will disappear with the suddenness and completeness of the flame of a candle that is blown out. All the agencies of inquisition—the hounds of the trail, the sleuths of the city's labyrinths, the closet detectives of theory and induction—will be invoked to the search. Most often the man's face will be seen no more. Sometimes he will reappear in Sheboygan or in the wilds of Terre Haute, calling himself one of the synonyms of "Smith," and without memory of events up to a certain time, including his grocer's bill. Sometimes it will be found, after dragging the rivers, and polling the restaurants to see if he may be waiting for a well-done sirloin, that he has moved next door.

This snuffing out of a human being like the erasure of a chalk man from a blackboard is one of the most impressive themes in dramaturgy.

The case of Mary Snyder, in point, should not be without interest.

A man of middle age, of the name of Meeks, came from the West to New York to find his sister, Mrs. Mary Snyder, a widow, aged fifty-two, who had been living for a year in a tenement house in a crowded neighbourhood.

At her address he was told that Mary Snyder had moved away longer than a month before. No one could tell him her new address.

On coming out Mr. Meeks addressed a policeman who was standing on the corner, and explained his dilemma.

"My sister is very poor," he said, "and I am anxious to find her. I have recently made quite a lot of money in a lead mine, and I want her to share my prosperity. There is no use in advertising her, because she cannot read."

The policeman pulled his moustache and looked so thoughtful and mighty that Meeks could almost feel the joyful tears of his sister Mary dropping upon his bright blue tie.

"You go down in the Canal Street neighbourhood," said the policeman, "and get a job drivin' the biggest dray you can find. There's old women always gettin' knocked

over by drays down there. You might see
'er among 'em. If you don't want to do that
you better go 'round to headquarters and get
'em to put a fly cop onto the dame."

At police headquarters Meeks received
ready assistance. A general alarm was sent
out, and copies of a photograph of Mary
Snyder that her brother had were distributed
among the stations. In Mulberry Street
the chief assigned Detective Mullins to the
case.

The detective took Meeks aside and said:

"This is not a very difficult case to unravel.
Shave off your whiskers, fill your pockets with
good cigars, and meet me in the café of the
Waldorf at three o'clock this afternoon."

Meeks obeyed. He found Mullins there.
They had a bottle of wine, while the detective
asked questions concerning the missing woman.

"Now," said Mullins, "New York is a big
city, but we've got the detective business
systematized. There are two ways we can go
about finding your sister. We will try one of
'em first. You say she's fifty-two?"

"A little past," said Meeks.

The detective conducted the Westerner to
a branch advertising office of one of the largest

dailies. There he wrote the following "ad" and submitted it to Meeks.

"Wanted, at once—one hundred attractive chorus girls for a new musical comedy. Apply all day at No.——— Broadway."

Meeks was indignant.

"My sister," said he, "is a poor, hard-working, elderly woman. I do not see what aid an advertisement of this kind would be toward finding her."

"All right," said the detective. "I guess you don't know New York. But if you've got a grouch against this scheme we'll try the other one. It's a sure thing. But it'll cost you more."

"Never mind the expense," said Meeks; "we'll try it."

The sleuth led him back to the Waldorf. "Engage a couple of bedrooms and a parlour," he advised, "and let's go up."

This was done, and the two were shown to a superb suite on the fourth floor. Meeks looked puzzled. The detective sank into a velvet armchair, and pulled out his cigar case.

"I forgot to suggest, old man," he said, "that you should have taken the rooms by the month. They wouldn't have stuck you so much for 'em."

"By the month!" exclaimed Meeks. "What do you mean?"

"Oh, it'll take time to work the game this way. I told you it would cost you more. We'll have to wait till spring. There'll be a new city directory out then. Very likely your sister's name and address will be in it."

Meeks rid himself of the city detective at once. On the next day some one advised him to consult Shamrock Jolnes, New York's famous private detective, who demanded fabulous fees, but performed miracles in the way of solving mysteries and crimes.

After waiting for two hours in the anteroom of the great detective's apartment, Meeks was shown into his presence. Jolnes sat in a purple dressing-gown at an inlaid ivory chess table, with a magazine before him, trying to solve the mystery of "They." The famous sleuth's thin, intellectual face, piercing eyes, and rate per word are too well known to need description.

Meeks set forth his errand. "My fee, if successful, will be $500," said Shamrock Jolnes.

Meeks bowed his agreement to the price.

"I will undertake your case, Mr. Meeks," said Jolnes finally. "The disappearance of people in this city has always been an interesting problem to me. I remember a case that I brought to a successful outcome a year ago. A family bearing the name of Clark disappeared suddenly from a small flat in which they were living. I watched the flat building for two months for a clue. One day it struck me that a certain milkman and a grocer's boy always walked backward when they carried their wares upstairs. Following out by induction the idea that this observation gave me, I at once located the missing family. They had moved into the flat across the hall and changed their name to Kralc."

Shamrock Jolnes and his client went to the tenement house where Mary Snyder had lived, and the detective demanded to be shown the room in which she had lived. It had been occupied by no tenant since her disappearance.

The room was small, dingy, and poorly furnished. Meeks seated himself dejectedly on a broken chair, while the great detective searched the walls and floor and the few sticks of old, rickety furniture for a clue.

At the end of half an hour Jolnes had collected a few seemingly unintelligible articles—
a cheap black hatpin, a piece torn off a
theatre programme, and the end of a small
torn card on which was the word "left" and
the characters "C 12."

Shamrock Jolnes leaned against the mantel
for ten minutes, with his head resting upon
his hand, and an absorbed look upon his intellectual face. At the end of that time he
exclaimed, with animation:

"Come, Mr. Meeks; the problem is solved.
I can take you directly to the house where
your sister is living. And you may have no
fears concerning her welfare, for she is amply
provided with funds—for the present at least."

Meeks felt joy and wonder in equal pro-
portions.

"How did you manage it?" he asked, with
admiration in his tones.

Perhaps Jolnes's only weakness was a professional pride in his wonderful achievements
in induction. He was ever ready to astound
and charm his listeners by describing his
methods.

"By elimination," said Jolnes, spreading
his clues upon a little table, "I got rid of cer-

tain parts of the city to which Mrs. Snyder might have removed. You see this hatpin? That eliminates Brooklyn. No woman attempts to board a car at the Brooklyn Bridge without being sure that she carries a hatpin with which to fight her way into a seat. And now I will demonstrate to you that she could not have gone to Harlem. Behind this door are two hooks in the wall. Upon one of these Mrs. Snyder has hung her bonnet, and upon the other her shawl. You will observe that the bottom of the hanging shawl has gradually made a soiled streak against the plastered wall. The mark is clean-cut, proving that there is no fringe on the shawl. Now, was there ever a case where a middle-aged woman, wearing a shawl, boarded a Harlem train without there being a fringe on the shawl to catch in the gate and delay the passengers behind her? So we eliminate Harlem.

"Therefore I conclude that Mrs. Snyder has not moved very far away. On this torn piece of card you see the word 'Left,' the letter 'C,' and the number '12.' Now, I happen to know that No. 12 Avenue C is a first-class boarding house, far beyond your sister's means—as we suppose. But then I find this piece of a theatre programme, crumpled into an odd shape. What meaning does it convey? None to you, very likely, Mr. Meeks; but it is eloquent to one whose habits and training take cognizance of the smallest things.

"You have told me that your sister was a scrub woman. She scrubbed the floors of offices and hallways. Let us assume that she procured such work to perform in a theatre. Where is valuable jewellery lost the oftenest, Mr. Meeks? In the theatres, of course. Look at that piece of programme, Mr. Meeks. Observe the round impression in it. It has been wrapped around a ring—perhaps a ring of great value. Mrs. Snyder found the ring while at work in the theatre. She hastily tore off a piece of a programme, wrapped the ring carefully, and thrust it into her bosom. The next day she disposed of it, and, with her increased means, looked about her for a more comfortable place in which to live. When I reach thus far in the chain I see nothing impossible about No. 12 Avenue C. It is there we will find your sister, Mr. Meeks."

Shamrock Jolnes concluded his convincing speech with the smile of a successful artist.

Meeks's admiration was too great for words.
Together they went to No. 12 Avenue C.
It was an old-fashioned brownstone house in a
prosperous and respectable neighbourhood.

They rang the bell, and on inquiring were
told that no Mrs. Snyder was known there,
and that not within six months had a new
occupant come to the house.

When they reached the sidewalk again,
Meeks examined the clues which he had
brought away from his sister's old room.

"I am no detective," he remarked to Jolnes
as he raised the piece of theatre programme to
his nose, "but it seems to me that instead
of a ring having been wrapped in this paper
it was one of those round peppermint drops.
And this piece with the address on it looks to
me like the end of a seat coupon—No. 12, row
C, left aisle."

Shamrock Jolnes had a far-away look in
his eyes.

"I think you would do well to consult
Juggins," said he.

"Who is Juggins?" asked Meeks.

"He is the leader," said Jolnes, "of a new
modern school of detectives. Their methods
are different from ours, but it is said that

Juggins has solved some extremely puzzling
cases. I will take you to him."

They found the greater Juggins in his office.
He was a small man with light hair, deeply
absorbed in reading one of the bourgeois
works of Nathaniel Hawthorne.

The two great detectives of different schools
shook hands with ceremony, and Meeks was
introduced.

"State the facts," said Juggins, going on
with his reading.

When Meeks ceased, the greater one closed
his book and said:

"Do I understand that your sister is fifty-
two years of age, with a large mole on the side
of her nose, and that she is a very poor widow,
making a scanty living by scrubbing, and with
a very homely face and figure?"

"That describes her exactly," admitted
Meeks. Juggins rose and put on his hat.

"In fifteen minutes," he said, "I will return, bringing you her present address."

Shamrock Jolnes turned pale, but forced a
smile.

Within the specified time Juggins returned and
consulted a little slip of paper held in his hand.

"Your sister, Mary Snyder," he announced

calmly, "will be found at No. 162 Chilton Street. She is living in the back hall bedroom, five flights up. The house is only four blocks from here," he continued, addressing Meeks. "Suppose you go and verify the statement and then return here. Mr. Jolnes will await you, I dare say."

Meeks hurried away. In twenty minutes he was back again, with a beaming face.

"She is there and well!" he cried. "Name your fee!"

"Two dollars," said Juggins.

When Meeks had settled his bill and departed, Shamrock Jolnes stood with his hat in his hand before Juggins.

"If it would not be asking too much," he stammered—"if you would favour me so far—would you object to——"

"Certainly not," said Juggins pleasantly. "I will tell you how I did it. You remember the description of Mrs. Snyder? Did you ever know a woman like that who wasn't paying weekly instalments on an enlarged crayon portrait of herself? The biggest factory of that kind in the country is just around the corner. I went there and got her address off the books. That's all."

XII

THE COP AND THE ANTHEM

ON HIS bench in Madison Square Soapy moved uneasily. When wild geese honk high of nights, and when women without sealskin coats grow kind to their husbands, and when Soapy moves uneasily on his bench in the park, you may know that winter is near at hand.

A dead leaf fell in Soapy's lap. That was Jack Frost's card. Jack is kind to the regular denizens of Madison Square, and gives fair warning of his annual call. At the corners of four streets he hands his pasteboard to the North Wind, footman of the mansion of All Outdoors, so that the inhabitants thereof may make ready.

Soapy's mind became cognizant of the fact that the time had come for him to resolve himself into a singular Committee of Ways and Means to provide against the coming rigour. And therefore he moved uneasily on his bench.

The hibernatorial ambitions of Soapy were not of the highest. In them there were no considerations of Mediterranean cruises, of soporific Southern skies, or drifting in the Vesuvian Bay. Three months on the Island was what his soul craved. Three months of assured board and bed and congenial company, safe from Boreas and bluecoats, seemed to Soapy the essence of things desirable.

For years the hospitable Blackwell's had been his winter quarters. Just as his more fortunate fellow New Yorkers had bought their tickets to Palm Beach and the Riviera each winter, so Soapy had made his humble arrangements for his annual hegira to the Island. And now the time was come. On the previous night three Sabbath newspapers, distributed beneath his coat, about his ankles, and over his lap, had failed to repulse the cold as he slept on his bench near the spurting fountain in the ancient square. So the Island loomed big and timely in Soapy's mind. He scorned the provisions made in the name of charity for the city's dependents. In Soapy's opinion the Law was more benign than Philanthropy. There was an endless round of institutions, municipal and eleemosy-

nary, on which he might set out and receive
lodging and food accordant with the simple
life. But to one of Soapy's proud spirit
the gifts of charity are encumbered. If not
in coin you must pay in humiliation of spirit
for every benefit received at the hands of
philanthropy. As Cæsar had his Brutus,
every bed of charity must have its toll of a
bath, every loaf of bread its compensation of
a private and personal inquisition. Wherefore it is better to be a guest of the law, which,
though conducted by rules, does not meddle
unduly with a gentleman's private affairs.

Soapy, having decided to go to the Island,
at once set about accomplishing his desire.
There were many easy ways of doing this.
The pleasantest was to dine luxuriously at
some expensive restaurant; and then, after
declaring insolvency, be handed over quietly
and without uproar to a policeman. An
accommodating magistrate would do the
rest.

Soapy left his bench and strolled out of the
square and across the level sea of asphalt,
where Broadway and Fifth Avenue flow together. Up Broadway he turned, and halted
at a glittering café, where are gathered to-

gether nightly the choicest products of the grape, the silkworm, and the protoplasm.

Soapy had confidence in himself from the lowest button of his vest upward. He was shaven, and his coat was decent and his neat, black, ready-tied four-in-hand had been presented to him by a lady missionary on Thanksgiving Day. If he could reach a table in the restaurant unsuspected success would be his. The portion of him that would show above the table would raise no doubt in the waiter's mind. A roasted mallard duck, thought Soapy, would be about the thing—with a bottle of Chablis, and then Camembert, a demi-tasse and a cigar. One dollar for the cigar would be enough. The total would not be so high as to call forth any supreme manifestation of revenge from the café management; and yet the meat would leave him filled and happy for the journey to his winter refuge.

But as Soapy set foot inside the restaurant door the head waiter's eye fell upon his frayed trousers and decadent shoes. Strong and ready hands turned him about and conveyed him in silence and haste to the sidewalk and averted the ignoble fate of the menaced mallard.

Soapy turned off Broadway. It seemed that his route to the coveted island was not to be an epicurean one. Some other way of entering limbo must be thought of.

At a corner of Sixth Avenue electric lights and cunningly displayed wares behind plate-glass made a shop window conspicuous. Soapy took a cobblestone and dashed it through the glass. People came running around the corner, a policeman in the lead. Soapy stood still, with his hands in his pockets, and smiled at the sight of brass buttons.

"Where's the man that done that?" inquired the officer excitedly.

"Don't you figure out that I might have had something to do with it?" said Soapy, not without sarcasm, but friendly, as one greets good fortune.

The policeman's mind refused to accept Soapy even as a clue. Men who smash windows do not remain to parley with the law's minions. They take to their heels. The policeman saw a man halfway down the block running to catch a car. With drawn club he joined in the pursuit. Soapy, with disgust in his heart, loafed along, twice unsuccessful.

On the opposite side of the street was a

restaurant of no great pretensions. It catered
to large appetites and modest purses. Its
crockery and atmosphere were thick; its soup
and napery thin. Into this place Soapy took
his accusive shoes and telltale trousers without challenge. At a table he sat and con-
sumed beefsteak, flapjacks, doughnuts, and
pie. And then to the waiter he betrayed the
fact that the minutest coin and himself were
strangers.

"Now, get busy and call a cop," said
Soapy. "And don't keep a gentleman waiting."

"No cop for youse," said the waiter, with a
voice like butter cakes and an eye like the
cherry in a Manhattan cocktail. "Hey,
Con!"

Neatly upon his left ear on the callous pave-
ment two waiters pitched Soapy. He arose,
joint by joint, as a carpenter's rule opens, and
beat the dust from his clothes. Arrest seemed
but a rosy dream. The Island seemed very
far away. A policeman who stood before a
drug store two doors away laughed and walked
down the street.

Five blocks Soapy travelled before his
courage permitted him to woo capture again.

This time the opportunity presented what he fatuously termed to himself a "cinch." A young woman of a modest and pleasing guise was standing before a show window gazing with sprightly interest at its display of shaving mugs and inkstands, and two yards from the window a large policeman of severe demeanour leaned against a water plug.

It was Soapy's design to assume the rôle of the despicable and execrated "masher." The refined and elegant appearance of his victim and the contiguity of the conscientious cop encouraged him to believe that he would soon feel the pleasant official clutch upon his arm that would insure his winter quarters on the right little, tight little isle.

Soapy straightened the lady missionary's ready-made tie, dragged his shrinking cuffs into the open, set his hat at a killing cant, and sidled toward the young woman. He made eyes at her, was taken with sudden coughs and "hems," smiled, smirked, and went brazenly through the impudent and contemptible litany of the "masher." With half an eye Soapy saw that the policeman was watching him fixedly. The young woman moved away a few steps, and again bestowed her absorbed

attention upon the shaving mugs. Soapy
followed, boldly stepping to her side, raised
his hat and said:

"Ah there, Bedelia! Don't you want to
come and play in my yard?"

The policeman was still looking. The per-
secuted young woman had but to beckon a
finger and Soapy would be practically en
route for his insular haven. Already he
imagined he could feel the cozy warmth of
the station-house. The young woman faced
him and, stretching out a hand, caught Soapy's
coat sleeve.

"Sure, Mike," she said joyfully— "if you'll
blow me to a pail of suds. I'd have spoke to
you sooner, but the cop was watching."

With the young woman playing the clinging
ivy to his oak Soapy walked past the policeman overcome with gloom. He seemed doomed
to liberty.

At the next corner he shook off his companion and ran. He halted in the district
where by night are found the lightest streets,
hearts, vows, and librettos. Women in furs
and men in greatcoats moved gaily in the
wintry air. A sudden fear seized Soapy that
some dreadful enchantment had rendered

him immune to arrest. The thought brought
a little of panic upon it, and when he came upon
another policeman lounging grandly in front
of a transplendent theatre he caught at the
immediate straw of "disorderly conduct."

On the sidewalk Soapy began to yell
drunken gibberish at the top of his harsh
voice. He danced, howled, raved, and otherwise disturbed the welkin.

The policeman twirled his club, turned his
back to Soapy, and remarked to a citizen:

"'Tis one of them Yale lads celebratin' the
goose egg they give to the Hartford College.
Noisy; but no harm. We've instructions to
lave them be."

Disconsolate, Soapy ceased his unavailing
racket. Would never a policeman lay hands
on him? In his fancy the Island seemed an
unattainable Arcadia. He buttoned his thin
coat against the chilling wind.

In a cigar store he saw a well-dressed man
lighting a cigar at a swinging light. His silk
umbrella he had set by the door on entering.
Soapy stepped inside, secured the umbrella,
and sauntered off with it slowly The man
at the cigar light followed hastily.

"My umbrella," he said sternly.

"Oh, is it?" sneered Soapy, adding insult to petit larceny. "Well, why don't you call a policeman? I took it. Your umbrella! Why don't you call a cop? There stands one on the corner."

The umbrella owner slowed his steps. Soapy did likewise, with a presentiment that luck would again run against him. The policeman looked at the two curiously.

"Of course," said the umbrella man—"that is—well, you know how these mistakes occur—I—if it's your umbrella I hope you'll excuse me—I picked it up this morning in a restaurant—if you recognize it as yours, why —I hope you'll——"

"Of course it's mine," said Soapy viciously.

The ex-umbrella man retreated. The policeman hurried to assist a tall blonde in an opera cloak across the street in front of a street car that was approaching two blocks away.

Soapy walked eastward through a street damaged by improvements. He hurled the umbrella wrathfully into an excavation. He muttered against the men who wear helmets and carry clubs. Because he wanted to fall into their clutches, they seemed to regard him as a king who could do no wrong.

At length Soapy reached one of the avenues to the east where the glitter and turmoil was but faint. He set his face down this toward Madison Square, for the homing instinct survives even when the home is a park bench.

But on an unusually quiet corner Soapy came to a standstill. Here was an old church, quaint and rambling and gabled. Through one violet-stained window a soft light glowed, where, no doubt, the organist loitered over the keys, making sure of his mastery of the coming Sabbath anthem. For there drifted out to Soapy's ears sweet music that caught and held him transfixed against the convolutions of the iron fence.

The moon was above, lustrous and serene; vehicles and pedestrians were few; sparrows twittered sleepily in the eaves—for a little while the scene might have been a country churchyard. And the anthem that the organist played cemented Soapy to the iron fence, for he had known it well in the days when his life contained such things as mothers and roses and ambitions and friends and immaculate thoughts and collars.

The conjunction of Soapy's receptive state of mind and the influences about the old church wrought a sudden and wonderful change in his soul. He viewed with swift horror the pit into which he had tumbled, the degraded days, unworthy desires, dead hopes, wrecked faculties, and base motives that made up his existence.

And also in a moment his heart responded thrillingly to this novel mood. An instantaneous and strong impulse moved him to battle with his desperate fate. He would pull himself out of the mire; he would make a man of himself again; he would conquer the evil that had taken possession of him. There was time; he was comparatively young yet; he would resurrect his old eager ambitions and pursue them without faltering. Those solemn but sweet organ notes had set up a revolution in him. To-morrow he would go into the roaring downtown district and find work. A fur importer had once offered him a place as driver. He would find him to-morrow and ask for the position. He would be somebody in the world. He would——

Soapy felt a hand laid on his arm. He

looked quickly around into the broad face of a policeman.

"What are you doin' here?" asked the officer.

"Nothin'," said Soapy.

"Then come along," said the policeman.

"Three months on the Island," said the Magistrate in the Police Court the next morning.

XIII

THE FOREIGN POLICY OF COMPANY 99

John Byrnes, hose-cart driver of Engine Company No. 99, was afflicted with what his comrades called Japanitis.

Byrnes had a war map spread permanently upon a table in the second story of the engine-house, and he could explain to you at any hour of the day or night the exact positions, conditions, and intentions of both the Russian and Japanese armies. He had little clusters of pins stuck in the map which represented the opposing forces, and these he moved about from day to day in conformity with the war news in the daily papers.

Wherever the Japs won a victory John Byrnes would shift his pins, and then he would execute a war dance of delight, and the other firemen would hear him yell: "Go it, you blamed little, sawed-off, huckleberry-eyed, monkey-faced hot tamales! Eat 'em up, you little sleight-o'-hand, bow-legged bull

terriers—give 'em another of them Yalu
looloos, and you'll eat rice in St. Petersburg.
Talk about your Russians—say, wouldn't
they give you a painsky when it comes to a
scrapovitch?"

Not even on the fair island of Nippon was
there a more enthusiastic champion of the
Mikado's men. Supporters of the Russian
cause did well to keep clear of Engine House
No. 99.

Sometimes all thoughts of the Japs left
John Byrnes's head. That was when the
alarm of fire had sounded and he was strapped
in his driver's seat on the swaying cart, guiding
Erebus and Joe, the finest team in the whole
department—according to the crew of 99.

Of all the codes adopted by man for regulat-
ing his actions toward his fellow-mortals, the
greatest are these—the code of King Arthur's
Knights of the Round Table, the Constitution of the United States, and the unwritten
rules of the New York Fire Department. The
Round Table methods are no longer prac-
ticable since the invention of street cars and
breach-of-promise suits, and our Constitution
is being found more and more unconstitu-
tional every day, so the code of our firemen

must be considered in the lead, with the
Golden Rule and Jeffries's new punch trying
for place and show.

The Constitution says that one man is as
good as another; but the Fire Department
says he is better. This is a too generous
theory, but the law will not allow itself to be
construed otherwise. All of which comes
perilously near to being a paradox, and com-
mends itself to the attention of the S. P. C. A.

One of the transatlantic liners dumped out
at Ellis Island a lump of protozoa which was
expected to evolve into an American citizen.
A steward kicked him down the gangway, a
doctor pounced upon his eyes like a raven,
seeking for trachoma or ophthalmia; he was
hustled ashore and ejected into the city in
the name of Liberty—perhaps, theoretically,
thus inoculating against kingocracy with a
drop of its own virus. This hypodermic in-
jection of Europeanism wandered happily
into the veins of the city with the broad grin
of a pleased child. It was not burdened with
baggage, cares, or ambitions. Its body was
lithely built and clothed in a sort of foreign
fustian; its face was brightly vacant, with a
small, flat nose, and was mostly covered by a

thick, ragged, curling beard like the coat of a
spaniel.   In the pocket of the imported Thing
were a few coins—denarii—scudi—kopecks—
pfennigs—pilasters—whatever the financial
nomenclature of his unknown country may
have been.

Prattling to himself, always broadly grinning, pleased by the roar and movement of
the barbarous city into which the steamship
cut-rates had shunted him, the alien strayed
away from the sea, which he hated, as far as
the district covered by Engine Company
No. 99.   Light as a cork, he was kept bobbing
along by the human tide, the crudest atom in
all the silt of the stream that emptied into
the reservoir of Liberty.

While crossing Third Avenue he slowed his
steps, enchanted by the thunder of the elevated trains above him and the soothing crash
of the wheels on the cobbles. And then
there was a new, delightful chord in the uproar—the musical clanging of a gong and a
great shining juggernaut belching fire and
smoke, that people were hurrying to see.

This beautiful thing, entrancing to the eye,
dashed past, and the protoplasmic immigrant
stepped into the wake of it with his broad,

enraptured, uncomprehending grin. And so stepping, stepped into the path of No. 99's flying hose-cart, with John Byrnes gripping, with arms of steel, the reins over the plunging backs of Erebus and Joe.

The unwritten constitutional code of the fireman has no exceptions or amendments. It is a simple thing—as simple as the rule of three. There was the heedless unit in the right of way; there was the hose-cart and the iron pillar of the elevated railroad.

John Byrnes swung all his weight and muscle on the left rein. The team and cart swerved that way and crashed like a torpedo into the pillar. The men on the cart went flying like skittles. The driver's strap burst, the pillar rang with the shock, and John Byrnes fell on the car track with a broken shoulder, twenty feet away, while Erebus—beautiful, raven-black, best-loved Erebus—lay whickering in his harness with a broken leg.

In consideration for the feelings of Engine Company No. 99 the details will be lightly touched. The company does not like to be reminded of that day. There was a great crowd, and hurry calls were sent in; and while the ambulance gong was clearing the way the

men of No. 99 heard the crack of the S. P.
C. A. agent's pistol, and turned their heads
away, not daring to look toward Erebus again.

When the firemen got back to the engine-
house they found that one of them was dragging by the collar the cause of their desolation
and grief. They set it in the middle of the
floor and gathered grimly about it. Through
its whiskers the calamitous object chattered
effervescently and waved its hands.

"Sounds like a seidlitz powder," said Mike
Dowling, disgustedly, "and it makes me
sicker than one. Call that a man!—that
hoss was worth a steamer full of such two-
legged animals. It's a immigrant—that's
what it is."

"Look at the doctor's chalk mark on its
coat," said Reilly, the desk man. "It's just
landed. It must be a kind of a Dago or a
Hun or one of them Finns, I guess. That's the
kind of truck that Europe unloads onto us."

"Think of a thing like that getting in the
way and laying John up in hospital and spoiling the best fire team in the city," groaned
another fireman. "It ought to be taken
down to the dock and drowned."

"Somebody go around and get Sloviski,"

suggested the engine driver, "and let's see what nation is responsible for this conglomeration of hair and head noises."

Sloviski kept a delicatessen store around the corner on Third Avenue, and was reputed to be a linguist.

One of the men fetched him—a fat, cringing man, with a discursive eye and the odours of many kinds of meats upon him.

"Take a whirl at this importation with your jawbreakers, Sloviski," requested Mike Dowling. "We can't quite figure out whether he's from the Hackensack bottoms or Hongkong-on-the-Ganges."

Sloviski addressed the stranger in several dialects, that ranged in rhythm and cadence from the sounds produced by a tonsillitis gargle to the opening of a can of tomatoes with a pair of scissors. The immigrant replied in accents resembling the uncorking of a bottle of ginger ale.

"I have you his name," reported Sloviski. "You shall not pronounce it. Writing of it in paper is better." They gave him paper, and he wrote, "Demetre Svangvsk."

"Looks like short hand," said the desk man.

"He speaks some language," continued the

interpreter, wiping his forehead, "of Austria and mixed with a little Turkish. And, den, he have some Magyar words and a Polish or two, and many like the Roumanian, but not without talk of one tribe in Bessarabia. I do not him quite understand."

"Would you call him a Dago or a Polocker, or what?" asked Mike, frowning at the polyglot description.

"He is a"—answered Sloviski—"he is a—I dink he come from—I dink he is a fool," he concluded, impatient at his linguistic failure, "and if you pleases I will go back at mine delicatessen."

"Whatever he is, he's a bird," said Mike Dowling; "and you want to watch him fly."

Taking by the wing the alien fowl that had fluttered into the nest of Liberty, Mike led him to the door of the engine-house and bestowed upon him a kick hearty enough to convey the entire animus of Company 99. Demetre Svangvsk hustled away down the sidewalk, turning once to show his ineradicable grin to the aggrieved firemen.

In three weeks John Byrnes was back at his post from the hospital. With great gusto he proceeded to bring his war map up to date.

"My money on the Japs every time," he declared. "Why, look at them Russians—they're nothing but wolves. Wipe 'em out, I say—and the little old jiu jitsu gang are just the cherry blossoms to do the trick, and don't you forget it!"

The second day after Byrnes's reappearance came Demetre Svangvsk, the unidentified, to the engine-house with a broader grin than ever. He managed to convey the idea that he wished to congratulate the hose-cart driver on his recovery and to apologize for having caused the accident. This he accomplished by so many extravagant gestures and explosive noises that the company was diverted for half an hour. Then they kicked him out again, and on the next day he came back grinning. How or where he lived no one knew. And then John Byrnes's nine-year-old son Chris, who brought him convalescent delicacies from home to eat, took a fancy to Svangvsk, and they allowed him to loaf about the door of the engine-house occasionally.

One afternoon the big drab automobile of the Deputy Fire Commissioner buzzed up to the door of No. 99 and the Deputy stepped inside for an informal inspection. The men kicked Svangvsk out a little harder than usual and proudly escorted the Deputy around 99, in which everything shone like my lady's mirror.

The Deputy respected the sorrow of the company concerning the loss of Erebus, and he had come to promise it another mate for Joe that would do him credit. So they let Joe out of his stall and showed the Deputy how deserving he was of the finest mate that could be in horsedom.

While they were circling around Joe confabbing, Chris climbed into the Deputy's auto and threw the power full on. The men heard a monster puffing and a shriek from the lad, and sprang out too late. The big auto shot away, luckily taking a straight course down the street. The boy knew nothing of its machinery; he sat clutching the cushions and howling. With the power on nothing could have stopped that auto except a brick house, and there was nothing for Chris to gain by such a stoppage.

Demetre Svangvsk was just coming in again with a grin for another kick when Chris played his merry little prank. While the others sprang for the door Demetre sprang for Joe. He glided upon the horse's bare back like a snake and shouted something at him like the crack of a dozen whips. One of the firemen afterward swore that Joe answered him back in the same language. Ten seconds after the auto started the big horse was eating up the asphalt behind it like a strip of macaroni.

Some people two blocks and a half away saw the rescue. They said that the auto was nothing but a drab noise with a black speck in the middle of it for Chris, when a big bay horse with a lizard lying on its back cantered up alongside of it, and the lizard reached over and picked the black speck out of the noise.

Only fifteen minutes after Svangvsk's last kicking at the hands—or rather the feet—of Engine Company No. 99 he rode Joe back through the door with the boy safe, but acutely conscious of the licking he was going to receive.

Svangvsk slipped to the floor, leaned his head against Joe's, and made a noise like a clucking hen. Joe nodded and whistled loudly through his nostrils, putting to shame the knowledge of Sloviski, of the delicatessen.

John Byrnes walked up to Svangvsk, who grinned, expecting to be kicked. Byrnes gripped the outlander so strongly by the hand that Demetre grinned anyhow, conceiving it to be a new form of punishment.

"The heathen rides like a Cossack," remarked a fireman who had seen a Wild West show—"they're the greatest riders in the world."

The word seemed to electrify Svangvsk. He grinned wider than ever.

"Yas—yas—me Cossack," he spluttered, striking his chest.

"Cossack!" repeated John Byrnes, thoughtfully, "ain't that a kind of a Russian?"

"They're one of the Russian tribes, sure," said the desk man, who read books between fire alarms.

Just then Alderman Foley, who was on his way home and did not know of the runaway, stopped at the door of the engine-house and called to Byrnes:

"Hello, there, Jimmy, me boy—how's the war coming along? Japs still got the bear on the trot, have they?"

"Oh, I don't know," said John Byrnes, argumentatively, "them Japs haven't got any walkover. You wait till Kuropatkin gets a good whack at 'em and they won't be knee-high to a puddle-ducksky."

XIV

MEMOIRS OF A YELLOW DOG

I DON'T suppose it will knock any of you
people off your perch to read a contribution
from an animal. Mr. Kipling and a good
many others have demonstrated the fact
that animals can express themselves in re-
munerative English, and no magazine goes
to press nowadays without an animal story
in it, except the old-style monthlies that are
still running pictures of Bryan and the Mont
Pelée horror.

But you needn't look for any stuck-up
literature in my piece, such as Bearoo, the
bear, and Snakoo, the snake, and Tammanoo,
the tiger, talk in the jungle books. A yellow
dog that's spent most of his life in a cheap
New York flat, sleeping in a corner on an old
sateen underskirt (the one she spilled port
wine on at the Lady 'Longshoremen's ban-
quet), mustn't be expected to perform any
tricks with the art of speech.

I was born a yellow pup; date, locality, pedigree, and weight unknown. The first thing I can recollect, an old woman had me in a basket at Broadway and Twenty-third trying to sell me to a fat lady. Old Mother Hubbard was boosting me to beat the band as a genuine Pomeranian-Hambletonian-Red-Irish-Cochin-China-Stoke-Pogis fox terrier. The fat lady chased a V around among the samples of gros grain flannelette in her shopping bag till she cornered it, and gave up. From that moment I was a pet—a mamma's own wootsey squidlums. Say, gentle reader, did you ever have a 200-pound woman breathing a flavour of Camembert cheese and Peau d'Espagne pick you up and wallop her nose all over you, remarking all the time in an Emma Eames tone of voice: "Oh, oo's um oodlum, doodlum, woodlum, toodlum, bitsy-witsy skoodlums?"

From a pedigreed yellow pup I grew up to be an anonymous yellow cur looking like a cross between an Angora cat and a box of lemons. But my mistress never tumbled. She thought that the two primeval pups that Noah chased into the ark were but a col-lateral branch of my ancestors. It took two

policemen to keep her from entering me at
the Madison Square Garden for the Siberian
bloodhound prize.

I'll tell you about that flat. The house was
the ordinary thing in New York, paved with
Parian marble in the entrance hall and cobble-
stones above the first floor. Our flat was
three fl—well, not flights—climbs up. My
mistress rented it unfurnished, and put in
the regular things—1903 antique unholstered
parlour set, oil chromo of geishas in a Harlem
tea house, rubber plant, and husband.

By Sirius! there was a biped I felt sorry
for. He was a little man with sandy hair and
whiskers a good deal like mine. Henpecked?
—well, toucans and flamingoes and pelicans
all had their bills in him. He wiped the
dishes and listened to my mistress tell about
the cheap, ragged things the lady with the
squirrel-skin coat on the second floor hung
out on her line to dry. And every evening
while she was getting supper she made him
take me out on the end of a string for a
walk.

If men knew how women pass the time
when they are alone they'd never marry.
Laura Lean Jibbey, peanut brittle, a little

almond cream on the neck muscles, dishes
unwashed, half an hour's talk with the ice-
man, reading a package of old letters, a
couple of pickles and two bottles of malt extract, one hour peeking through a hole in
the window shade into the flat across the
air-shaft—that's about all there is to it.
Twenty minutes before time for him to
come home from work she straightens up
the house, fixes her rat so it won't show,
and gets out a lot of sewing for a ten-minute
bluff.

I led a dog's life in that flat. 'Most all
day I lay there in my corner watching that
fat woman kill time. I slept sometimes and
had pipe dreams about being out chasing
cats into basements and growling at old ladies
with black mittens, as a dog was intended
to do. Then she would pounce upon me
with a lot of that drivelling poodle palaver
and kiss me on the nose—but what could I
do? A dog can't chew cloves.

I began to feel sorry for Hubby, dog my
cats if I didn't. We looked so much alike
that people noticed it when we went out; so
we shook the streets that Morgan's cab drives
down, and took to climbing the piles of last

December's snow on the streets where cheap people live.

One evening when we were thus promenading, and I was trying to look like a prize St. Bernard, and the old man was trying to look like he wouldn't have murdered the first organ-grinder he heard play Mendelssohn's wedding-march, I looked up at him and said, in my way:

"What are you looking so sour about, you oakum trimmed lobster? She don't kiss you. You don't have to sit on her lap and listen to talk that would make the book of a musical comedy sound like the maxims of Epictetus. You ought to be thankful you're not a dog. Brace up, Benedick, and bid the blues begone."

The matrimonial mishap looked down at me with almost canine intelligence in his face.

"Why, doggie," says he, "good doggie. You almost look like you could speak. What is it, doggie—Cats?"

Cats! Could speak!

But, of course, he couldn't understand. Humans were denied the speech of animals. The only common ground of communication upon which dogs and men can get together is in fiction.

In the flat across the hall from us lived a lady with a black-and-tan terrier. Her husband strung it and took it out every evening, but he always came home cheerful and whistling. One day I touched noses with the black-and-tan in the hall, and I struck him for an elucidation.

"See here, Wiggle-and-Skip," I says, "you know that it ain't the nature of a real man to play dry nurse to a dog in public. I never saw one leashed to a bow-wow yet that didn't look like he'd like to lick every other man that looked at him. But your boss comes in every day as perky and set up as an amateur prestidigitator doing the egg trick. How does he do it? Don't tell me he likes it."

"Him?" says the black-and-tan. "Why, he uses Nature's Own Remedy. He gets spifflicated. At first when we go out he's as shy as the man on the steamer who would rather play pedro when they make 'em all jackpots. By the time we've been in eight saloons he don't care whether the thing on the end of his line is a dog or a catfish. I've lost two inches of my tail trying to sidestep those swinging doors."

The pointer I got from that terrier—vaudeville please copy—set me to thinking.

One evening about 6 o'clock my mistress
ordered him to get busy and do the ozone act
for Lovey. I have concealed it until now,
but that is what she called me. The black-
and-tan was called "Tweetness." I consider
that I have the bulge on him as far as you
could chase a rabbit. Still "Lovey" is something of a nomenclatural tin can on the tail
of one's self-respect.

At a quiet place on a safe street I tightened
the line of my custodian in front of an attractive, refined saloon. I made a dead-
ahead scramble for the doors, whining like
a dog in the press despatches that lets the
family know that little Alice is bogged while
gathering lilies in the brook.

"Why, darn my eyes," says the old man,
with a grin; "darn my eyes if the saffron-
coloured son of a seltzer lemonade ain't asking me in to take a drink. Lemme see—
how long's it been since I saved shoe leather
by keeping one foot on the foot-rest? I
believe I'll——"

I knew I had him. Hot Scotches he took,
sitting at a table. For an hour he kept the

Campbells coming. I sat by his side rapping for the waiter with my tail, and eating free lunch such as mamma in her flat never equalled with her homemade truck bought at a delicatessen store eight minutes before papa comes home.

When the products of Scotland were all exhausted except the rye bread the old man unwound me from the table leg and played me outside like a fisherman plays a salmon. Out there he took off my collar and threw it into the street.

"Poor doggie," says he; "good doggie. She shan't kiss you any more. 'S a darned shame. Good doggie, go away and get run over by a street car and be happy."

I refused to leave. I leaped and frisked around the old man's legs happy as a pug on a rug.

"You old flea-headed woodchuck-chaser," I said to him—"you moon-baying, rabbit-pointing, egg-stealing old beagle, can't you see that I don't want to leave you? Can't you see that we're both Pups in the Wood and the missis is the cruel uncle after you with the dish towel and me with the flea liniment and a pink bow to tie on my tail.

Why not cut that all out and be pards forever more?"

Maybe you'll say he didn't understand—maybe he didn't. But he kind of got a grip on the Hot Scotches, and stood still for a minute, thinking.

"Doggie," says he, finally, "we don't live more than a dozen lives on this earth, and very few of us live to be more than 500. If I ever see that flat any more I'm a flat, and if you do you're flatter; and that's no flattery. I'm offering 60 to 1 that Westward Ho wins out by the length of a dachshund."

There was no string, but I frolicked along with my master to the Twenty-third Street ferry. And the cats on the route saw reason to give thanks that prehensile claws had been given them.

On the Jersey side my master said to a stranger who stood eating a currant bun:

"Me and my doggie, we are bound for the Rocky Mountains."

But what pleased me most was when my old man pulled both of my ears until I howled, and said:

"You common, monkey-headed, rat-tailed

sulphur-coloured son of a door mat, do you know what I'm going to call you?"

I thought of "Lovey," and I whined dolefully.

"I'm going to call you 'Pete,'" says my master; and if I'd had five tails I couldn't have done enough wagging to do justice to the occasion.

XV

LOST ON DRESS PARADE

Mr. Towers Chandler was pressing his evening suit in his hall bedroom. One iron was heating on a small gas stove; the other was being pushed vigorously back and forth to make the desirable crease that would be seen later on extending in straight lines from Mr. Chandler's patent leather shoes to the edge of his low-cut vest. So much of the hero's toilet may be intrusted to our confidence. The remainder may be guessed by those whom genteel poverty has driven to ignoble expedient. Our next view of him shall be as he descends the steps of his lodging-house immaculately and correctly clothed; calm, assured, handsome—in appearance the typical New York young clubman setting out, slightly bored, to inaugurate the pleasures of the evening.

Chandler's honorarium was $18 per week. He was employed in the office of an architect.

He was twenty-two years old; he considered
architecture to be truly an art; and he honestly
believed—though he would not have dared
to admit it in New York—that the Flatiron
Building was inferior in design to the great
cathedral in Milan.

Out of each week's earnings Chandler set
aside $1. At the end of each ten weeks with
the extra capital thus accumulated, he purchased one gentleman's evening from the
bargain counter of stingy old Father Time.
He arrayed himself in the regalia of million-
aires and presidents; he took himself to the
quarter where life is brightest and showiest,
and there dined with taste and luxury. With
ten dollars a man may, for a few hours, play
the wealthy idler to perfection. The sum is
ample for a well-considered meal, a bottle
bearing a respectable label, commensurate
tips, a smoke, cab fare, and the ordinary
etcetras.

This one delectable evening culled from
each dull seventy was to Chandler a source
of renascent bliss. To the society bud comes
but one début; it stands alone sweet in her
memory when her hair has whitened; but to
Chandler each ten weeks brought a joy as

keen, as thrilling, as new as the first had
been.   To sit among *bon vivants* under palms in
the swirl of concealed music, to look upon the
habitués of such a paradise and to be looked
upon by them—what is a girl's first dance and
short-sleeved tulle compared with this?

Up Broadway Chandler moved with the
vespertine dress parade.   For this evening he
was an exhibit as well as a gazer.   For the
next sixty-nine evenings he would be dining
in cheviot and worsted at dubious *table
d'hôtes*, at whirlwind lunch counters, on sand-
wiches and beer in his hall bedroom.   He was
willing to do that, for he was a true son of the
great city of razzle-dazzle, and to him one
evening in the limelight made up for many
dark ones.

Chandler protracted his walk until the
Forties began to intersect the great and
glittering primrose way, for the evening was
yet young, and when one is of the *beau
monde* only one day in seventy, one loves to
protract the pleasure. Eyes bright, sinister,
curious, admiring, provocative, alluring were
bent upon him, for his garb and air proclaimed him a devotee to the hour of solace
and pleasure.

At a certain corner he came to a standstill, proposing to himself the question of turning back toward the showy and fashionable restaurant in which he usually dined on the evenings of his especial luxury. Just then a girl scudded lightly around the corner, slipped on a patch of icy snow, and fell plump upon the sidewalk.

Chandler assisted her to her feet with instant and solicitous courtesy. The girl hobbled to the wall of the building, leaned against it, and thanked him demurely.

"I think my ankle is strained," she said. "It twisted when I fell."

"Does it pain you much?" inquired Chandler.

"Only when I rest my weight upon it. I think I will be able to walk in a minute or two."

"If I can be of any further service," suggested the young man, "I will call a cab, or——"

"Thank you," said the girl, softly but heartily. "I am sure you need not trouble yourself any further. It was so awkward of me. And my shoe heels are horridly common-sense: I can't blame them at all."

Chandler looked at the girl and found her
swiftly drawing his interest. She was pretty
in a refined way; and her eye was both
merry and kind. She was inexpensively clothed
in a plain black dress that suggested a sort
of uniform such as shop girls wear. Her
glossy dark-brown hair showed its coils beneath a cheap hat of black straw whose only
ornament was a velvet ribbon and bow. She
could have posed as a model for the self-
respecting working girl of the best type.

A sudden idea came into the head of the
young architect. He would ask this girl to
dine with him. Here was the element that
his splendid but solitary periodic feasts had
lacked. His brief season of elegant luxury
would be doubly enjoyable if he could add to
it a lady's society. This girl was a lady, he
was sure—her manner and speech settled
that. And in spite of her extremely plain
attire he felt that he would be pleased to sit
at table with her.

These thoughts passed swiftly through his
mind, and he decided to ask her. It was a
breach of etiquette, of course, but oftentimes
wage-earning girls waived formalities in matters of this kind. They were generally

shrewd judges of men; and thought better of
their own judgment than they did of useless
conventions. His ten dollars, discreetly ex-
pended, would enable the two to dine very
well indeed. The dinner would no doubt be
a wonderful experience thrown into the dull
routine of the girl's life; and her lively ap-
preciation of it would add to his own triumph
and pleasure.

"I think," he said to her, with frank
gravity, "that your foot needs a longer rest
than you suppose. Now, I am going to
suggest a way in which you can give it that
and at the same time do me a favour. I was
on my way to dine all by my lonely self when
you came tumbling around the corner. You
come with me and we'll have a cozy dinner
and a pleasant talk together, and by that
time your game ankle will carry you home
very nicely, I am sure."

The girl looked quickly up into Chandler's
clear, pleasant countenance. Her eyes
twinkled once very brightly, and then she
smiled ingenuously.

"But we don't know each other—it would-
n't be right, would it?" she said doubtfully.

"There is nothing wrong about it," said

the young man candidly. "I'll introduce myself—permit me—Mr. Towers Chandler. After our dinner, which I will try to make as pleasant as possible, I will bid you good-evening, or attend you safely to your door, whichever you prefer."

"But, dear me!" said the girl, with a glance at Chandler's faultless attire. "In this old dress and hat!"

"Never mind that," said Chandler cheerfully. "I'm sure you look more charming in them than any one we shall see in the most elaborate dinner toilette."

"My ankle does hurt yet," admitted the girl, attempting a limping step. "I think I will accept your invitation, Mr. Chandler. You may call me—Miss Marian."

"Come, then, Miss Marian," said the young architect, gaily, but with perfect courtesy; "you will not have far to walk. There is a very respectable and good restaurant in the next block. You will have to lean on my arm—so—and walk slowly. It is lonely dining all by one's self. I'm just a little bit glad that you slipped on the ice."

When the two were established at a well-appointed table, with a promising waiter hovering in attendance, Chandler began to experience the real joy that his regular outing always brought to him.

The restaurant was not so showy or pretentious as the one farther down Broadway, which he always preferred, but it was nearly so.   The tables were well filled with prosperous-looking diners, there was a good orchestra, playing softly enough to make conversation a possible pleasure, and the cuisine and service were beyond criticism. His companion, even in her cheap hat and dress, held herself with an air that added distinction to the natural beauty of her face and figure.   And it is certain that she looked at Chandler, with his animated but self-possessed manner and his kindling and frank blue eyes, with something not far from admiration in her own charming face.

Then it was that the Madness of Manhattan, the Frenzy of Fuss and Feathers, the Bacillus of Brag, the Provincial Plague of Pose seized upon Towers Chandler. He was on Broadway, surrounded by pomp and style, and there were eyes to look at him. On the stage of that comedy he had assumed to play the one-night part of a butterfly of

fashion and an idler of means and taste. He
was dressed for the part, and all his good
angels had not the power to prevent him
from acting it.

So he began to prate to Miss Marian of
clubs, of teas, of golf and riding and kennels
and cotillions and tours abroad and threw
out hints of a yatch lying at Larchmont. He
could see that she was vastly impressed by
this vague talk, so he endorsed his pose by
random insinuations concerning great wealth,
and mentioned familiarly a few names that
are handled reverently by the proletariat. It
was Chandler's short little day, and he was
wringing from it the best that could be had,
as he saw it. And yet once or twice he saw
the pure gold of this girl shine through the
mist that his egotism had raised between
him and all objects.

"This way of living that you speak of," she
said, "sounds so futile and purposeless.
Haven't you any work to do in the world
that might interest you more?"

"My dear Miss Marian," he exclaimed—
"work! Think of dressing every day for
dinner, of making half a dozen calls in an
afternoon—with a policeman at every corner

ready to jump into your auto and take you
to the station if you get up any greater
speed than a donkey cart's gait. We do-
nothings are the hardest workers in the
land."

The dinner was concluded, the waiter
generously feed, and the two walked out to
the corner where they had met. Miss Marian
walked very well now; her limp was scarcely
noticeable.

"Thank you for a nice time," she said
frankly. "I must run home now. I liked
the dinner very much, Mr. Chandler."

He shook hands with her, smiling cordially,
and said something about a game of bridge
at his club. He watched her for a moment,
walking rather rapidly eastward, and then he
found a cab to drive him slowly homeward.

In his chilly bedroom Chandler laid away
his evening clothes for a sixty-nine days' rest.
He went about it thoughtfully.

"That was a stunning girl," he said to
himself. "She's all right, too, I'd be sworn,
even is she does have to work. Perhaps if
I'd told her the truth instead of all that
razzle-dazzle we might—but, confound it! I
had to play up to my clothes."

Thus spoke the brave who was born and reared in the wigwams of the tribe of the Manhattans.

The girl, after leaving her entertainer, sped swiftly cross-town until she arrived at a handsome and sedate mansion two squares to the east, facing on that avenue which is the highway of Mammon and the auxiliary gods. Here she entered hurriedly and ascended to a room where a handsome young lady in an elaborate house dress was looking anxiously out the window.

"Oh, you, madcap!" exclaimed the elder girl, when the other entered. "When will you quit frightening us this way? It is two hours since you ran out in that rag of an old dress and Marie's hat. Mamma has been so alarmed. She sent Louis in the auto to try to find you. You are a bad, thoughtless Puss."

The elder girl touched a button, and a maid came in a moment.

"Marie, tell mamma that Miss Marian has returned."

"Don't scold, sister. I only ran down to Mme. Theo's to tell her to use mauve insertion instead of pink. My costume and

Marie's hat were just what I needed. Every one thought I was a shopgirl, I am sure."

"Dinner is over, dear; you stayed so late."

"I know. I slipped on the sidewalk and turned my ankle. I could not walk, so I hobbled into a restaurant and sat there until I was better. That is why I was so long."

The two girls sat in the window seat, looking out at the lights and the stream of hurrying vehicles in the avenue. The younger one cuddled down with her head in her sister's lap.

"We will have to marry some day," she said dreamily—"both of us. We have so much money that we will not be allowed to disappoint the public. Do you want me to tell you the kind of a man I could love, Sis?"

"Go on, you scatterbrain," smiled the other.

"I could love a man with dark and kind blue eyes, who is gentle and respectful to poor girls, who is handsome and good and does not try to flirt. But I could love him only if he had an ambition, an object, some work to do in the world. I would not care how poor he was if I could help him build his way up. But, sister dear, the kind of man we always

meet—the man who lives an idle life between
society and his clubs—I could not love a
man like that, even if his eyes were blue and
he were ever so kind to poor girls whom he
met in the street."

XVI

THE LOVE-PHILTRE OF IKEY SCHOENSTEIN

The Blue Light Drug Store is downtown, between the Bowery and First Avenue, where the distance between the two streets is the shortest. The Blue Light does not consider that pharmacy is a thing of bric-a-brac, scent, and ice-cream soda. If you ask it for pain-killer it will not give you a bonbon.

The Blue Light scorns the labour-saving arts of modern pharmacy. It macerates its opium and percolates its own laudanum and paregoric. To this day pills are made behind its tall prescription desk—pills rolled out on its own pill-tile, divided with a spatula, rolled with the finger and thumb, dusted with calcined magnesia, and delivered in little round pasteboard pill-boxes. The store is on a corner about which coveys of ragged-plumed, hilarious children play and become candidates for the cough drops and soothing syrups that wait for them inside.

Ikey Schoenstein was the night clerk of the Blue Light and the friend of his customers. Thus it is on the East Side, where the heart of pharmacy is not glacé. There, as it should be, the druggist is a counsellor, a confessor, an adviser, an able and willing missionary and mentor whose learning is respected, whose occult wisdom is venerated, and whose medicine is often poured, untasted, into the gutter. Therefore Ikey's corniform, be-spectacled nose and narrow, knowledge-bowed figure was well known in the vicinity of the Blue Light, and his advice and notice were much desired.

Ikey roomed and breakfasted at Mrs. Riddle's two squares away. Mrs. Riddle had a daughter named Rosy. The circumlocution has been in vain—you must have guessed it —Ikey adored Rosy. She tinctured all his thoughts; she was the compound extract of all that was chemically pure and officinal— the dispensatory contained nothing equal to her. But Ikey was timid, and his hopes remained insoluble in the menstruum of his backwardness and fears. Behind his counter he was a superior being, calmly conscious of special knowledge and worth; outside he was a weak-kneed, purblind, motorman-cursed rambler, with ill-fitting clothes stained with chemicals and smelling of socotrine aloes and valerianate of ammonia.

The fly in Ikey's ointment (thrice welcome, pat trope!) was Chunk McGowan.

Mr. McGowan was also striving to catch the bright smiles tossed about by Rosy. But he was no outfielder as Ikey was; he picked them off the bat. At the same time he was Ikey's friend and customer, and often dropped in at the Blue Light Drug Store to have a bruise painted with iodine or get a cut rubber-plastered after a pleasant evening spent along the Bowery.

One afternoon McGowan drifted in in his silent, easy way, and sat, comely, smooth-faced, hard, indomitable, good-natured, upon a stool.

"Ikey," said he, when his friend had fetched his mortar and sat opposite, grinding gum benzoin to a powder, "get busy with your ear. It's drugs for me if you've got the line I need."

Ikey scanned the countenance of Mr. McGowan for the usual evidences of conflict, but found none.

"Take your coat off," he ordered. "I

guess already that you have been stuck in the ribs with a knife. I have many times told you those Dagoes would do you up."

Mr. McGowan smiled. "Not them," he said. "Not any Dagoes. But you've located the diagnosis all right enough—it's under my coat, near the ribs. Say! Ikey—Rosy and me are goin' to run away and get married to-night."

Ikey's left forefinger was doubled over the edge of the mortar, holding it steady. He gave it a wild rap with the pestle, but felt it not. Meanwhile Mr. McGowan's smile faded to a look of perplexed gloom.

"That is," he continued, "if she keeps in the notion until the time comes. We've been layin' pipes for the getaway for two weeks. One day she says she will; the same evenin' she says nixy. We've agreed on to-night, and Rosy's stuck to the affirmative this time for two whole days. But it's five hours yet till the time, and I'm afraid she'll stand me up when it comes to the scratch."

"You said you wanted drugs," remarked Ikey.

Mr. McGowan looked ill at ease and ha-rassed—a condition opposed to his usual line of

demeanour. He made a patent-medicine al-
manac into a roll and fitted it with unprofitable carefulness about his finger.

"I wouldn't have this double handicap
make a false start to-night for a million," he
said. "I've got a little flat up in Harlem all
ready, with chrysanthemums on the table and
a kettle ready to boil. And I've engaged a
pulpit pounder to be ready at his house for us
at 9.30. It's got to come off. And if Rosy
don't change her mind again!"—Mr. Mc-
Gowan ceased, a prey to his doubts.

"I don't see then yet," said Ikey, shortly,
"what makes it that you talk of drugs, or
what I can be doing about it."

"Old man Riddle don't like me a little bit,"
went on the uneasy suitor, bent upon mar-
shalling his arguments. "For a week he
hasn't let Rosy step outside the door with
me. If it wasn't for losin' a boarder they'd
have bounced me long ago. I'm makin' $20
a week and she'll never regret flyin' the coop
with Chunk McGowan."

"You will excuse me, Chunk," said Ikey.
"I must make a prescription that is to be
called for soon."

"Say," said McGowan, looking up suddenly, "say, Ikey, ain't there a drug of some kind—some kind of powders that'll make a girl like you better if you give 'em to her?"

Ikey's lip beneath his nose curled with the scorn of superior enlightenment; but before he could answer, McGowan continued:

"Tim Lacy told me he got some once from a croaker uptown and fed 'em to his girl in soda water. From the very first dose he was ace-high and everybody else looked like thirty cents to her. They was married in less than two weeks."

Strong and simple was Chunk McGowan. A better reader of men than Ikey was could have seen that his tough frame was strung upon fine wires. Like a good general who was about to invade the enemy's territory he was seeking to guard every point against possible failure.

"I thought," went on Chunk hopefully, "that if I had one of them powders to give Rosy when I see her at supper to-night it might brace her up and keep her from reneging on the proposition to skip. I guess she don't need a mule team to drag her away, but women are better at coaching than they are at running bases. If the stuff'll work just for a couple of hours it'll do the trick."

"When is this foolishness of running away to be happening?" asked Ikey.

"Nine o'clock," said Mr. McGowan. "Supper's at seven. At eight Rosy goes to bed with a headache. At nine old Parvenzano lets me through to his backyard, where there's a board off Riddle's fence, next door. I go under her window and help her down the fire-escape. We've got to make it early on the preacher's account. It's all dead easy if Rosy don't balk when the flag drops. Can you fix one of them powders, Ikey?"

Ikey Schoenstein rubbed his nose slowly.

"Chunk," said he, "it is of drugs of that nature that pharmaceutists must have much carefulness. To you alone of my acquaintance would I intrust a powder like that. But for you I shall make it, and you shall see how it makes Rosy to think of you."

Ikey went behind the prescription desk. There he crushed to a powder two soluble tablets, each containing a quarter of a grain of morphia. To them he added a little sugar of milk to increase the bulk, and folded the mixture neatly in a white paper. Taken by an adult this powder would insure several hours of heavy slumber without danger to the sleeper. This he handed to Chunk Mc-Gowan, telling him to administer it in a liquid if possible, and received the hearty thanks of the backyard Lochinvar.

The subtlety of Ikey's action becomes apparent upon recital of his subsequent move. He sent a messenger for Mr. Riddle and disclosed the plans of Mr. McGowan for eloping with Rosy. Mr. Riddle was a stout man, brick-dusty of complexion and sudden in action.

"Much obliged," he said, briefly, to Ikey. "The lazy Irish loafer! My own room's just above Rosy's. I'll just go up there myself after supper and load the shot-gun and wait. If he comes in my backyard he'll go away in a ambulance instead of a bridal chaise."

With Rosy held in the clutches of Morpheus for a many-hours deep slumber, and the bloodthirsty parent waiting, armed and forewarned, Ikey felt that his rival was close, indeed, upon discomfiture.

All night in the Blue Light Drug Store he

waited at his duties for chance news of the tragedy, but none came.

At eight o'clock in the morning the day clerk arrived and Ikey started hurriedly for Mrs. Riddle's to learn the outcome. And, lo! as he stepped out of the store who but Chunk McGowan sprang from a passing street car and grasped his hand—Chunk McGowan with a victor's smile and flushed with joy.

"Pulled it off," said Chunk with Elysium in his grin. "Rosy hit the fire-escape on time to a second, and we was under the wire at the Reverend's at 9.30¼. She's up at the flat—she cooked eggs this mornin' in a blue kimono—Lord! how lucky I am! You must pace up some day, Ikey, and feed with us. I've got a job down near the bridge, and that's where I'm heading for now."

"The—the—powder?" stammered Ikey.

"Oh, that stuff you gave me!" said Chunk, broadening his grin; "well, it was this way. I sat down at the supper table last night at Riddle's, and I looked at Rosy, and I says to myself, 'Chunk, if you get the girl get her on the square—don't try any hocus-pocus with a thoroughbred like her.' And I keeps the paper you give me in my pocket. And then my lamps fall on another party present, who, I says to myself, is failin' in a proper affection toward his comin' son-in-law, so I watches my chance and dumps that powder in old man Riddle's coffee—see?"

XVII

THE GIRL AND THE HABIT

HABIT—a tendency or aptitude acquired by custom
or frequent repetition.

THE critics have assailed every source of
inspiration save one. To that one we are
driven for our moral theme. When we levied
upon the masters of old they gleefully dug
up the parallels to our columns. When we
strove to set forth real life they reproached us
for trying to imitate Henry George, George
Washington, Washington Irving, and Irving
Bacheller. We wrote of the West and the
East, and they accused us of both Jesse and
Henry James. We wrote from our heart—
and they said something about a disordered
liver. We took a text from Matthew or—er—
yes, Deuteronomy, but the preachers were
hammering away at the inspiration idea
before we could get into type. So, driven
to the wall, we go for our subject-matter to

the reliable, old, moral, unassailable **vade mecum**—the unabridged dictionary.

Miss Merriam was cashier at Hinkle's. Hinkle's was one of the big downtown restaurants. It is in what the papers call the "financial district." Each day from 12 o'clock to 2 Hinkle's was full of hungry customers— messenger boys, stenographers, brokers, owners of mining stock, promoters, inventors with patents pending—and also people with money.

The cashier at Hinkle's was no sinecure. Hinkle egged and toasted and griddle-caked and coffeed a good many customers; and he lunched (as good a word as "dined") many more. It might be said that Hinkle's breakfast crowd was a contingent, but his luncheon patronage amounted to a horde.

Miss Merriam sat on a stool at a desk inclosed on three sides by a strong, high fencing of woven brass wire. Through an arched opening at the bottom you thrust your waiter's check and the money, while your heart went pit-a-pat.

For Miss Merriam was lovely and capable. She could take 45 cents out of a $2 bill and refuse an offer of marriage before you could——

Next!—lost your chance—please don't shove.
She could keep cool and collected while she
collected your check, give you the correct
change, win you heart, indicate the tooth-
pick stand, and rate you to a quarter of a
cent better than Bradstreet could to a thousand in less time than it takes to pepper an
egg with one of Hinkle's casters.

There is an old and dignified allusion to the
"fierce light that beats upon a throne." The
light that beats upon the young lady cashier's
cage is also something fierce.   The other fellow is responsible for the slang.

Every male patron of Hinkle's, from the
A. D. T. boys up to the curbstone brokers,
adored Miss Merriam.   When they paid
their checks they wooed her with every wile
known to Cupid's art.   Between the meshes
of the brass railing went smiles, winks,
compliments, tender vows, invitations to
dinner, sighs, languishing looks, and merry
banter that was wafted pointedly back by the
gifted Miss Merriam.

There is no coign of vantage more effective
than the position of young lady cashier.   She
sits there, easily queen of the court of com-
merce; she is duchess of dollars and devoirs,

countess of compliments and coin, leading lady of love and luncheon. You take from her a smile and a Canadian dime, and you go your way uncomplaining. You count the cheery word or two that she tosses you as misers count their treasures; and you pocket the change for a five uncomputed. Perhaps the brass-bound inaccessibility multiplies her charms—anyhow, she is a shirt-waisted angel, immaculate, trim, manicured, seductive, bright-eyed, ready, alert—Psyche, Circe, and Ate in one, separating you from your circulating medium after your sirloin medium.

The young men who broke bread at Hinkle's never settled with the cashier without an exchange of badinage and open compliment. Many of them went to greater lengths and dropped promissory hints of theatre tickets and chocolates. The older men spoke plainly of orange blossoms, generally withering the tentative petals by after-allusions to Harlem flats. One broker who had been squeezed by copper proposed to Miss Merriam more regularly than he ate.

During a brisk luncheon hour Miss Merriam's conversation, while she took money for checks, would run something like this:

"Good morning, Mr. Haskins—sir?—it's natural, thank you—don't be quite so fresh . . . Hello, Johnny—ten, fifteen, twenty —chase along now or they'll take the letters off your cap . . . Beg pardon—count it again, please—Oh, don't mention it . . . Vaudeville?—thanks; not on your moving picture—I was to see Carter in Hedda Gabler on Wednesday night with Mr. Simmons . . . 'Scuse me, I thought that was a quarter . . . Twenty-five and seventy-five's a dollar—got that ham-and-cabbage habit yet. I see, Billy . . . Who are you addressing?— say—you'll get all that's coming to you in a minute . . . Oh, fudge! Mr. Bassett— you're always fooling—no—? Well, maybe I'll marry you some day—three, four, and sixty-five is five . . . Kindly keep them remarks to yourself, if you please . . . Ten cents?—'scuse me; the check calls for seventy—well, maybe it is a one instead of a seven . . . Oh, do you like it that way, Mr. Saunders?—some prefer a pomp; but they say this Cleo de Merody does suit refined features . . . and ten is fifty . . . Hike along there, buddy; don't take this for

a Coney Island ticket booth . . . Huh?—
why, Macy's—don't it fit nice? Oh, no, it
isn't too cool—these light-weight fabrics is
all the go this season . . . Come again,
please—that's the third time you've tried to—
what?—forget it—that lead quarter is an old
friend of mine . . . Sixty-five?—must
have had your salary raised, Mr. Wilson
. . . I seen you on Sixth Avenue Tuesday
afternoon, Mr. De Forest—swell?—oh, my!—
who is she? . . . What's the matter
with it?—why, it ain't money—what?— Co-
lumbian half?—well, this ain't South America
. . . Yes, I like the mixed best—Friday?
—awfully sorry, but I take my jiu-jitsu
lesson on Friday—Thursday, then . . .
Thanks—that's sixteen times I've been told
that this morning—I guess I must be beautiful
. . . Cut that out, please—who do you
think I am? . . . Why, Mr. Westbrook
—do you really think so?—the idea!—one—
eighty and twenty's a dollar—thank you ever
so much; but I don't ever go automobile
riding with gentlemen—your aunt?—well,
that's different—perhaps . . . Please
don't get fresh—your check was fifteen cents,
I believe—kindly step aside and let . . .

Hello, Ben—coming around Thursday evening?—there's a gentleman going to send
around a box of chocolates, and . . .
forty and sixty is a dollar, and one is two
. . ."

About the middle of one afternoon the
dizzy goddess Vertigo—whose other name is
Fortune—suddenly smote an old, wealthy
and eccentric banker while he was walking
past Hinkle's, on his way to a street car. A
wealthy and eccentric banker who rides in
street cars is—move up, please; there are
others.

A Samaritan, a Pharisee, a man and a
policeman who were first on the spot lifted
Banker McRamsey and carried him into
Hinkle's restaurant. When the aged but
indestructible banker opened his eyes he saw
a beautiful vision bending over him with a
pitiful, tender smile, bathing his forehead
with beef tea and chafing his hands with
something frappé out of a chafing-dish. Mr.
McRamsey sighed, lost a vest button, gazed
with deep gratitude upon his fair preserveress,
and then recovered consciousness.

To the Seaside Library all who are anticipat-
ing a romance! Banker McRamsey had an

aged and respected wife, and his sentiments toward Miss Merriam were fatherly. He talked to her for half an hour with interest— not the kind that went with his talks during business hours. The next day he brought Mrs. McRamsey down to see her. The old couple were childless—they had only a married daughter living in Brooklyn.

To make a short story shorter, the beautiful cashier won the hearts of the good old couple. They came to Hinkle's again and again; they invited her to their old-fashioned but splendid home in one of the East Seventies. Miss Merriam's winning loveliness, her sweet frankness and impulsive heart took them by storm. They said a hundred times that Miss Merriam reminded them so much of their lost daughter. The Brooklyn matron, née Ramsey, had the figure of Buddha and a face like the ideal of an art photographer. Miss Merriam was a combination of curves, smiles, rose leaves, pearls, satin, and hair-tonic posters. Enough of the fatuity of parents.

A month after the worthy couple became acquainted with Miss Merriam she stood before Hinkle one afternoon and resigned her cashiership.

"They're going to adopt me," she told the bereft restaurateur. "They're funny old people, but regular dears. And the swell home they have got! Say, Hinkle, there isn't any use of talking—I'm on the à la carte to wear brown duds and goggles in a whiz wagon, or marry a duke at least. Still, I somehow hate to break out of the old cage. I've been cashiering so long I feel funny doing anything else. I'll miss joshing the fellows awfully when they line up to pay for the buckwheats and. But I can't let this chance slide. And they're awfully good, Hinkle; I know I'll have a swell time. You owe me nine-sixty-two and a half for the week. Cut out the half if it hurts you, Hinkle."

And they did. Miss Merriam became Miss Rosa McRamsey. And she graced the transition. Beauty is only skin-deep, but the nerves lie very near to the skin. Nerve— but just here will you oblige by perusing again the quotation with which this story begins?

The McRamseys poured out money like domestic champagne to polish their adopted one. Milliners, dancing masters, and private tutors got it. Miss—er—McRamsey was grateful, loving, and tried to forget Hinkle's. To give ample credit to the adaptability of the American girl, Hinkle's did fade from her memory and speech most of the time.

Not every one will remember when the Earl of Hitesbury came to East Seventy—— Street, America. He was only a fair-to-medium earl, without debts, and he created little excitement. But you will surely remember the evening when the Daughters of Benevolence held their bazaar in the W——f-A——a Hotel. For you were there, and you wrote a note to Fannie on the hotel paper, and mailed it, just to show her that—you did not? Very well; that was the evening the baby was sick, of course.

At the Bazaar the McRamseys were prominent. Miss Mer—er—McRamsey was exquisitely beautiful. The Earl of Hitesbury had been very attentive to her since he dropped in to have a look at America. At the charity bazaar the affair was supposed to be going to be pulled off to a finish. An earl is as good as a duke. Better. His standing may be lower, but his outstanding accounts are also lower.

Our ex-young-lady-cashier was assigned to

a booth. She was expected to sell worthless articles to nobs and snobs at exorbitant prices. The proceeds of the bazaar were to be used for giving to the poor children of the slums a Christmas din—— Say! did you ever wonder where they get the other 364?

Miss McRamsey—beautiful, palpitating, excited, charming, radiant—fluttered about in her booth. An imitation brass network, with a little arched opening, fenced her in.

Along came the Earl, assured, delicate, accurate, admiring—admiring greatly, and faced the open wicket.

"You look chawming, you know—'pon my word you do—my deah," he said beguilingly.

Miss McRamsey whirled around.

"Cut that joshing out," she said coolly and briskly. "Who do you think you are talking to? Your check, please. Oh, Lordy! ——"

Patrons of the bazaar became aware of a commotion and pressed around a certain booth. The Earl of Hitesbury stood near by pulling a pale blond and puzzled whisker.

"Miss McRamsey has fainted," some one explained.

XVIII

AFTER TWENTY YEARS

THE policeman on the beat moved up the avenue impressively. The impressiveness was habitual and not for show, for spectators were few. The time was barely 10 o'clock at night, but chilly gusts of wind with a taste of rain in them had well nigh depeopled the streets.

Trying doors as he went, twirling his club with many intricate and artful movements, turning now and then to cast his watchful eye adown the pacific thoroughfare, the officer, with his stalwart form and slight swagger, made a fine picture of a guardian of the peace. The vicinity was one that kept early hours. Now and then you might see the lights of a cigar store or of an all-night lunch counter; but the majority of the doors belonged to business places that had long since been closed.

When about midway of a certain block

the policeman suddenly slowed his walk. In
the doorway of a darkened hardware store
a man leaned, with an unlighted cigar in his
mouth. As the policeman walked up to
him the man spoke up quickly:

"It's all right, officer," he said reassuringly.
"I'm just waiting for a friend. It's an appointment made twenty years ago. Sounds a
little funny to you, doesn't it? Well, I'll explain if you'd like to make certain it's all
straight. About that long ago there used
to be a restaurant where this store stands
—'Big Joe' Brady's restaurant."

"Until five years ago," said the policeman.
"It was torn down then."

The man in the doorway struck a match
and lit his cigar. The light showed a pale,
square-jawed face with keen eyes, and a
little white scar near his right eyebrow. His
scarfpin was a large diamond, oddly set.

"Twenty years ago to-night," said the man,
"I dined here at 'Big Joe' Brady's with Jimmy
Wells, my best chum, and the finest chap in
the world. He and I were raised here in
New York, just like two brothers, together.
I was eighteen and Jimmy was twenty. The
next morning I was to start for the West to

make my fortune. You couldn't have dragged Jimmy out of New York; he thought it was the only place on earth. Well, we agreed that night that we would meet here again exactly twenty years from that date and time, no matter what our conditions might be or from what distance we might have to come. We figured that in twenty years each of us ought to have our destiny worked out and our fortunes made, whatever they were going to be."

"It sounds pretty interesting," said the policeman. "Rather a long time between meets, though, it seems to me. Haven't you heard from your friend since you left?"

"Well, yes, for a time we corresponded," said the other. "But after a year or two we lost track of each other. You see, the West is a pretty big proposition, and I kept hustling around over it pretty lively. But I know Jimmy will meet me here if he's alive, for he always was the truest, stanchest old chap in the world. He'll never forget. I came a thousand miles to stand in this door to-night, and it's worth it if my old partner turns up."

The waiting man pulled out a handsome watch, the lids of it set with small diamonds.

"Three minutes to ten," he announced. "It was exactly ten o'clock when we parted here at the restaurant door."

"Did pretty well out West, didn't you?" asked the policeman.

"You bet! I hope Jimmy has done half as well. He was a kind of plodder, though, good fellow as he was. I've had to compete with some of the sharpest wits going to get my pile. A man gets in a groove in New York. It takes the West to put a razor-edge on him."

The policeman twirled his club and took a step or two.

"I'll be on my way. Hope your friend comes around all right. Going to call time on him sharp?"

"I should say not!" said the other. "I'll give him half an hour at least. If Jimmy is alive on earth he'll be here by that time. So long, officer."

"Good-night, sir," said the policeman, passing on along his beat, trying doors as he went.

There was now a fine, cold drizzle falling, and the wind had risen from its uncertain puffs into a steady blow The few foot passengers astir in that quarter hurried dismally and silently along with coat collars turned high and pocketed hands. And in the door of the hardware store the man who had come a thousand miles to fill an appointment, uncertain almost to absurdity, with the friend of his youth, smoked his cigar and waited.

About twenty minutes he waited, and then a tall man in a long overcoat, with collar turned up to his ears, hurried across from the opposite side of the street. He went directly to the waiting man.

"Is that you, Bob?" he asked doubtfully.

"Is that you, Jimmy Wells?" cried the man in the door.

"Bless my heart!" exclaimed the new arrival, grasping both the other's hands with his own. "It's Bob, sure as fate. I was certain I'd find you here if you were still in existence. Well, well, well!—twenty years is a long time. The old restaurant's gone, Bob; I wish it had lasted, so we could have had another dinner there. How has the West treated you, old man?"

"Bully; it has given me everything I asked it for. You've changed lots, Jimmy. I never thought you were so tall by two or three inches."

"Oh, I grew a bit after I was twenty."

"Doing well in New York, Jimmy?"

"Moderately. I have a position in one of the city departments. Come on, Bob; we'll go around to a place I know of, and have a good long talk about old times."

The two men started up the street, arm in arm. The man from the West, his egotism enlarged by success, was beginning to outline the history of his career. The other, submerged in his overcoat, listened with interest.

At the corner stood a drug store, brilliant with electric lights. When they came into this glare each of them turned simultaneously to gaze upon the other's face.

The man from the West stopped suddenly and released his arm.

"You're not Jimmy Wells," he snapped. "Twenty years is a long time, but not long enough to change a man's nose from a Roman to a pug."

"It sometimes changes a good man into a bad one," said the tall man. "You've been under arrest for ten minutes, 'Silky' Bob. Chicago thinks you may have dropped over our way and wires us she wants to have a chat with you. Going quietly, are you? That's sensible. Now, before we go on to the station here's a note I was asked to hand you. You may read it here at the window. It's from Patrolman Wells."

The man from the West unfolded the little piece of paper handed him. His hand was steady when he began to read, but it trembled a little by the time he had finished. The note was rather short:

Bob: I was at the appointed place on time. When you struck the match to light your cigar I saw it was the face of the man wanted in Chicago. Somehow I couldn't do it myself, so I went around and got a plain clothes man to do the job.

JIMMY.

XIX

"WHAT YOU WANT"

Night had fallen on that great and beautiful city known as Bagdad-on-the-Subway. And with the night came the enchanted glamour that belongs not to Arabia alone. In different masquerade the streets, bazaars, and walled houses of the occidental city of romance were filled with the same kind of folk that so much interested our interesting old friend, the late Mr. H. A. Rashid. They wore clothes eleven hundred years nearer to the latest styles than H. A. saw in the old Bagdad; but they were about the same people underneath. With the eye of faith, you could have seen the Little Hunchback, Sinbad the Sailor, Fitbad the Tailor, the Beautiful Persian, the one-eyed Calenders, Ali Baba and Forty Robbers on every block, and the Barber and his Six Brothers, and all the old Arabian gang easily.

But let us revenue to our lamb chops.

Old Tom Crowley was a caliph. He had $42,000,000 in preferred stocks and bonds with solid gold edges. In these times, to be called a caliph you must have money. The old-style caliph business as conducted by Mr. Rashid is not safe. If you hold up a person nowadays in a bazaar or a Turkish bath or a side street, and inquire into his private and personal affairs, the police court'll get you.

Old Tom was tired of clubs, theatres, dinners, friends, music, money, and everything. That's what makes a caliph—you must get to despise everything that money can buy, and then go out and try to want something that you can't pay for.

"I'll take a little trot around town all by myself," thought old Tom, "and try if I can stir up anything new. Let's see—it seems I've read about a king or a Cardiff giant or something in old times who used to go about with false whiskers on, making Persian dates with folks he hadn't been introduced to. That don't listen like a bad idea. I certainly have got a case of humdrumness and fatigue on for the ones I do know. That old Cardiff used to pick up cases of trouble as he ran upon 'em and give 'em gold—sequins, I think it

was—and make 'em marry or got 'em good
Government jobs. Now, I'd like something
of that sort. My money is as good as his was
even if the magazines do ask me every month
where I got it. Yes, I guess I'll do a little
Cardiff business to-night, and see how it
goes."

Plainly dressed, old Tom Crowley left his
Madison Avenue palace, and walked westward and then south. As he stepped to the
sidewalk, Fate, who holds the ends of the
strings in the central offices of all the enchanted cities, pulled a thread, and a young
man twenty blocks away looked at a wall
clock, and then put on his coat.

James Turner worked in one of those little
hat-cleaning establishments on Sixth Avenue
in which a fire alarm rings when you push the
door open, and where they clean your hat
while you wait—two days. James stood all
day at an electric machine that turned hats
around faster than the best brands of champagne ever could have done. Overlooking
your mild impertinence in feeling a curiosity
about the personal appearance of a stranger,
I will give you a modified description of him.
Weight, 118; complexion, hair, and brain,

light; height, five feet six; age, about twenty-three; dressed in a $10 suit of greenish-blue serge; pockets containing two keys and sixty-three cents in change.

But do not misconjecture because this description sounds like a General Alarm that James was either lost or a dead one.

Allons!

James stood all day at his work. His feet were tender and extremely susceptible to impositions being put upon or below them. All day long they burned and smarted, causing him much suffering and inconvenience. But he was earning twelve dollars per week, which he needed to support his feet whether his feet would support him or not.

James Turner had his own conception of what happiness was, just as you and I have ours. Your delight is to gad about the world in yachts and motor-cars and to hurl ducats at wild fowl. Mine is to smoke a pipe at evenfall and watch a badger, a rattlesnake, and an owl go into their common prairie home one by one.

James Turner's idea of bliss was different; but it was his. He would go directly to his boarding-house when his day's work was done.

After his supper of small steak, Bessemer potatoes, stooed (not stewed) apples and infusion of chicory, he would ascend to his fifth-floor-back hall room. Then he would take off his shoes and socks, place the soles of his burning feet against the cold bars of his iron bed, and read Clark Russell's sea yarns. The delicious relief of the cool metal applied to his smarting soles was his nightly joy. His favourite novels never palled upon him; the sea and the adventures of its navigators were his sole intellectual passion. No millionaire was ever happier than James Turner taking his ease.

When James left the hat-cleaning shop he walked three blocks out of his way home to look over the goods of a second-hand book-stall. On the sidewalk stands he had more than once picked up a paper-covered volume of Clark Russell at half price.

While he was bending with a scholarly stoop over the marked-down miscellany of cast-off literature, old Tom the caliph sauntered by. His discerning eye, made keen by twenty years' experience in the manufacture of laundry soap (save the wrappers!) recognized instantly the poor and discerning scholar, a

worthy object of his caliphanous mood. He
descended the two shallow stone steps that
led from the sidewalk, and addressed without
hesitation the object of his designed mu-
nificence. His first words were no worse than
salutatory and tentative.

James Turner looked up coldly, with "Sar-
tor Resartus" in one hand and "A Mad
Marriage" in the other.

"Beat it," said he. "I don't want to buy
any coat hangers or town lots in Hankipoo,
New Jersey. Run along, now, and play with
your Teddy bear."

"Young man," said the caliph, ignoring
the flippancy of the hat cleaner, "I observe
that you are of a studious disposition. Learning is one of the finest things in the world. I
never had any of it worth mentioning, but I
admire to see it in others. I come from the
West, where we imagine nothing but facts.
Maybe I couldn't understand the poetry and
allusions in them books you are picking over,
but I like to see somebody else seem to know
what they mean. Now, I'd like to make you
a proposition. I'm worth about $40,000,000,
and I'm getting richer every day. I made
the height of it manufacturing Aunt Patty's

Silver Soap. I invented the art of making it. I experimented for three years before I got just the right quantity of chloride of sodium solution and caustic potash mixture to curdle properly. And after I had taken some $9,000,000 out of the soap business I made the rest in corn and wheat futures. Now, you seem to have the literary and scholarly turn of character; and I'll tell you what I'll do. I'll pay for your education at the finest college in the world. I'll pay the expense of your rummaging over Europe and the art galleries, and finally set you up in a good business. You needn't make it soap if you have any objections. I see by your clothes and frazzled necktie that you are mighty poor; and you can't afford to turn down the offer. Well, when do you want to begin?"

The hat cleaner turned upon old Tom the eye of the Big City, which is an eye expressive of cold and justifiable suspicion, of judgment suspended as high as Haman was hung, of self-preservation, of challenge, curiosity, defiance, cynicism, and, strange as you may think it, of a childlike yearning for friendliness and fellowship that must be hidden when one walks among the "stranger bands." For in

New Bagdad one, in order to survive, must suspect whosoever sits, dwells, drinks, rides, walks, or sleeps in the adjacent chair, house, booth, seat, path, or room.

"Say, Mike," said James Turner, "what's your line, anyway—shoe laces? I'm not buying anything. You better put an egg in your shoe and beat it before incidents occur to you. You can't work off any fountain pens, gold spectacles you found on the street, or trust company certificate house clearings on me. Say, do I look like I'd climbed down one of them missing fire-escapes at Helicon Hall? What's vitiating you, anyhow?"

"Son," said the caliph, in his most Harunish tones, "as I said, I'm worth $40,000,000. I don't want to have it all put in my coffin when I die. I want to do some good with it. I seen you handling over these here volumes of literature, and I thought I'd keep you. I've give the missionary societies $2,000,000, but what did I get out of it? Nothing but a receipt from the secretary. Now, you are just the kind of young man I'd like to take up and see what money could make of him."

Volumes of Clark Russell were hard to find

that evening at the Old Book Shop. And James Turner's smarting and aching feet did not tend to improve his temper. Humble hat cleaner though he was, he had a spirit equal to any caliph's.

"Say, you old faker," he said, angrily, "be on your way. I don't know what your game is, unless you want change for a bogus $40,000,000 bill. Well, I don't carry that much around with me. But I do carry a pretty fair left-handed punch that you'll get if you don't move on."

"You are a blamed impudent little gutter pup," said the caliph.

Then James delivered his self-praised punch; old Tom seized him by the collar and kicked him thrice; the hat cleaner rallied and clinched; two bookstands were overturned, and the books sent flying. A cop came up, took an arm of each, and marched them to the nearest station house. "Fighting and disorderly conduct," said the cop to the sergeant.

"Three hundred dollars bail," said the sergeant at once, asseveratingly and inquiringly.

"Sixty-three cents," said James Turner with a harsh laugh.

The caliph searched his pockets and collected small bills and change amounting to four dollars.

"I am worth," he said, "forty million dollars, but——"

"Lock 'em up," ordered the sergeant.

In his cell, James Turner laid himself on his cot, ruminating. "Maybe he's got the money, and maybe he ain't. But if he has or he ain't what does he want to go 'round butting into other folks's business for? When a man knows what he wants, and can get it, it's the same as $40,000,000 to him."

Then an idea came to him that brought a pleased look to his face.

He removed his socks, drew his cot close to the door, stretched himself out luxuriously, and placed his tortured feet against the cold bars of the cell door. Something hard and bulky under the blankets of his cot gave one shoulder discomfort. He reached under, and drew out a paper-covered volume by Clark Russell called "A Sailor's Sweetheart." He gave a great sigh of contentment.

Presently to his cell came the doorman and said:

"Say, kid, that old gazabo that was pinched

with you for scrapping seems to have been
the goods after all.   He 'phoned to his friends,
and he's out at the desk now with a roll of
yellowbacks as big as a Pullman car pillow.
He wants to bail you, and for you to come
out to see him."

"Tell him I ain't in," said James Turner.

XX

THE CLARION CALL

HALF of this story can be found in the records of the Police Department; the other half belongs behind the business counter of a newspaper office.

One afternoon two weeks after Millionaire Norcross was found in his apartment murdered by a burglar, the murderer, while strolling serenely down Broadway, ran plump against Detective Barney Woods.

"Is that you, Johnny Kernan?" asked Woods, who had been near-sighted in public for five years.

"No less," cried Kernan heartily. "If it isn't Barney Woods, late and early of old Saint Jo! You'll have to show me! What are you doing East? Do the green-goods circulars get out that far?"

"I've been in New York some years," said Woods. "I'm on the city detective force."

"Well, well!" said Kernan, breathing smiling joy and patting the detective's arm.

"Come into Muller's," said Woods, "and
let's hunt a quiet table. I'd like to talk to
you awhile."

It lacked a few minutes to the hour of four.
The tides of trade were not yet loosed, and
they found a quiet corner of the café. Kernan, well dressed, slightly swaggering, self-
confident, seated himself opposite the little
detective, with his pale, sandy moustache,
squinting eyes, and ready-made cheviot suit.

"What business are you in now?" asked
Woods. "You know you left Saint Jo a year
before I did."

"I'm selling shares in a copper mine," said
Kernan. "I may establish an office here.
Well, well! and so old Barney is a New York
detective. You always had a turn that way.
You were on the police in Saint Jo after I left
there, weren't you?"

"Six months," said Woods. "And now
there's one more question, Johnny. I've
followed your record pretty close ever since
you did that hotel job in Saratoga, and I
never knew you to use your gun before.
Why did you kill Norcross?"

Kernan stared for a few moments with con-
centrated attention at the slice of lemon in
his high-ball; and then he looked at the detective with a sudden, crooked, brilliant smile.

"How did you guess it, Barney?" he asked
admiringly. "I swear I thought the job was
as clean and as smooth as a peeled onion.
Did I leave a string hanging out anywhere?"

Woods laid upon the table a small gold
pencil intended for a watch-charm.

"It's the one I gave you the last Christmas
we were in Saint Jo. I've got your shaving
mug yet. I found this under a corner of the
rug in Norcross's room. I warn you to be
careful what you say. I've got it put on to
you, Johnny. We were old friends once, but
I must do my duty. You'll have to go to the
chair for Norcross."

Kernan laughed.

"My luck stays with me," said he.
"Who'd have thought old Barney was on
my trail!" He slipped one hand inside his
coat. In an instant Woods had a revolver
against his side.

"Put it away," said Kernan, wrinkling his
nose. "I'm only investigating. Aha! It
takes nine tailors to make a man. but one

can do a man up.   There's a hole in that vest
pocket.   I took that pencil off my chain and
slipped it in there in case of a scrap.   Put
up your gun, Barney, and I'll tell you why I
had to shoot Norcross.   The old fool started
down the hall after me, popping at the buttons on the back of my coat with a peevish
little .22 and I had to stop him.   The old
lady was a darling.   She just lay in bed and
saw her $12,000 diamond necklace go with-
out a chirp, while she begged like a pan-
handler to have back a little thin gold ring
with a garnet worth about $3.   I guess she
married old Norcross for his money, all
right.   Don't they hang on to the little
trinkets from the Man Who Lost Out, though?
There were six rings, two brooches, and a
chatelaine watch.   Fifteen thousand would
cover the lot."

"I warned you not to talk," said Woods.

"Oh, that's all right," said Kernan.   "The
stuff is in my suit case at the hotel.   And now
I'll tell you why I'm talking.   Because it's
safe.   I'm talking to a man I know.   You
owe me a thousand dollars, Barney Woods,
and even if you wanted to arrest me your
hand wouldn't make the move."

"I haven't forgotten," said Woods. "You counted out twenty fifties without a word. I'll pay it back some day. That thousand saved me and—well, they were piling my furniture out on the sidewalk when I got back to the house."

"And so," continued Kernan, "you being Barney Woods, born as true as steel, and bound to play a white man's game, can't lift a finger to arrest the man you're indebted to. Oh, I have to study men as well as Yale locks and window fastenings in my business. Now, keep quiet while I ring for the waiter. I've had a thirst for a year or two that worries me a little. If I'm ever caught the lucky sleuth will have to divide honours with old boy Booze. But I never drink during business hours. After a job I can crook elbows with my old friend Barney with a clear conscience. What are you taking?"

The waiter came with the little decanters and the siphon and left them alone again.

"You've called the turn," said Woods, as he rolled the little gold pencil about with a thoughtful forefinger. "I've got to pass you up. I can't lay a hand on you. If I'd a-paid that money back—but I didn't, and that settles it. It's a bad break I'm making, Johnny, but I can't dodge it. You helped me once, and it calls for the same."

"I knew it," said Kernan, raising his glass, with a flushed smile of self-appreciation. "I can judge men. Here's to Barney, for— 'he's a jolly good fellow.'"

"I don't believe," went on Woods quietly, as if he were thinking aloud, "that if accounts had been square between you and me, all the money in all the banks in New York could have bought you out of my hands to-night."

"I know it couldn't," said Kernan. "That's why I knew I was safe with you."

"Most people," continued the detective, "look sideways at my business. They don't class it among the fine arts and the professions. But I've always taken a kind of fool pride in it. And here is where I go 'busted.' I guess I'm a man first and a detective afterward. I've got to let you go, and then I've got to resign from the force. I guess I can drive an express wagon. Your thousand dollars is further off than ever, Johnny."

"Oh, you're welcome to it," said Kernan,

with a lordly air. "I'd be willing to call the
debt off, but I know you wouldn't have it.
It was a lucky day for me when you borrowed
it. And now, let's drop the subject. I'm
off to the West on a morning train. I know
a place out there where I can negotiate the
Norcross sparks. Drink up, Barney, and
forget your troubles. We'll have a jolly
time while the police are knocking their
heads together over the case. I've got one
of my Sahara thirsts on to-night. But I'm
in the hands—the unofficial hands—of my
old friend Barney, and I won't even dream of
a cop."

And then, as Kernan's ready finger kept
the button and the waiter working, his weak
point—a tremendous vanity and arrogant
egotism, began to show itself. He recounted
story after story of his successful plunderings,
ingenious plots and infamous transgressions
until Woods, with all his familiarity with
evil-doers, felt growing within him a cold ab-
horrence toward the utterly vicious man who
had once been his benefactor.

"I'm disposed of, of course," said Woods,
at length. "But I advise you to keep under
cover for a spell. The newspapers may take

up this Norcross affair. There has been an epidemic of burglaries and manslaughter in town this summer."

The word sent Kernan into a high glow of sullen and vindictive rage.

"To h—l with the newspapers," he growled. "What do they spell but brag and blow and boodle in box-car letters? Suppose they do take up a case—what does it amount to? The police are easy enough to fool; but what do the newspapers do? They send a lot of pin-head reporters around to the scene; and they make for the nearest saloon and have beer while they take photos of the bartender's oldest daughter in evening dress, to print as the fiancée of the young man in the tenth story, who thought he heard a noise below on the night of the murder. That's about as near as the newspapers ever come to running down Mr. Burglar."

"Well, I don't know," said Woods, reflecting. "Some of the papers have done good work in that line. There's the *Morning Mars*, for instance. It warmed up two or three trails, and got the man after the police had let 'em get cold."

"I'll show you," said Kernan, rising, and

expanding his chest. "I'll show you what I think of newspapers in general, and your *Morning Mars* in particular."

Three feet from their table was the telephone booth. Kernan went inside and sat at the instrument, leaving the door open. He found a number in the book, took down the receiver and made his demand upon Central. Woods sat still, looking at the sneering, cold, vigilant face waiting close to the transmitter, and listened to the words that came from the thin, truculent lips curved into a contemptuous smile.

"That the *Morning Mars?* . . . I want to speak to the managing editor . . . Why, tell him it's some one who wants to talk to him about the Norcross murder.

"You the editor? . . . All right. . . . I am the man who killed old Norcross . . . Wait! Hold the wire; I'm not the usual crank . . . Oh, there isn't the slightest danger. I've just been discussing it with a detective friend of mine. I killed the old man at 2:30 A. M. two weeks ago to-morrow . . . Have a drink with you? Now, hadn't you better leave that kind of talk to your funny man? Can't you tell whether a man's

guying you or whether you're being offered
the biggest scoop your dull dishrag of a paper
ever had? . . . Well, that's so; it's a bob-
tail scoop—but you can hardly expect me to
'phone in my name and address. . . .
Why? Oh, because I heard you make a
specialty of solving mysterious crimes that
stump the police. . . . No, that's not
all. I want to tell you that your rotten,
lying, penny sheet is of no more use in track-
ing an intelligent murderer or highwayman
than a blind poodle would be. . . . What?
. . . Oh, no, this isn't a rival newspaper
office; you're getting it straight. I did the
Norcross job, and I've got the jewels in my
suit case at—'the name of the hotel could
not be learned'—you recognize that phrase,
don't you? I thought so. You've used it
often enough. Kind of rattles you, doesn't
it, to have the mysterious villain call up your
great, big, all-powerful organ of right and justice and good government and tell you what a
helpless old gas-bag you are? . . . Cut
that out; you're not that big a fool—no, you
don't think I'm a fraud. I can tell it by your
voice. . . . Now, listen, and I'll give
you a pointer that will prove it to you. Of

course you've had this murder case worked over by your staff of bright young blockheads. Half of the second button on old Mrs. Norcross's nightgown is broken off. I saw it when I took the garnet ring off her finger. I thought it was a ruby. . . . Stop that! it won't work."

Kernan turned to Woods with a diabolic smile.

"I've got him going. He believes me now. He didn't quite cover the transmitter with his hand when he told somebody to call up Central on another 'phone and get our number. I'll give him just one more dig, and then we'll make a 'get-away.'

"Hello! . . . Yes. I'm here yet. You didn't think I'd run from such a little subsidized, turncoat rag of a newspaper, did you? . . . Have me inside of forty-eight hours? Say, will you quit being funny? Now, you let grown men alone and attend to your business of hunting up divorce cases and street-car accidents and printing the filth and scandal that you make your living by. Good-bye, old boy—sorry I haven't time to call on you. I'd feel perfectly safe in your sanctum asinorum. Tra-la!"

"He's as mad as a cat that's lost a mouse," said Kernan, hanging up the receiver and coming out. "And now, Barney, my boy, we'll go to a show and enjoy ourselves until a reasonable bedtime. Four hours' sleep for me, and then the west-bound."

The two dined in a Broadway restaurant. Kernan was pleased with himself. He spent money like a prince of fiction. And then a weird and gorgeous musical comedy engaged their attention. Afterward there was a late supper in a grillroom, with champagne, and Kernan at the height of his complacency.

Half-past three in the morning found them in a corner of an all-night café, Kernan still boasting in a vapid and rambling way, Woods thinking moodily over the end that had come to his usefulness as an upholder of the law.

But, as he pondered, his eye brightened with a speculative light.

"I wonder if it's possible," he said to himself, "I won-der if it's pos-si-ble!"

And then outside the café the comparative stillness of the early morning was punctured by faint, uncertain cries that seemed mere fireflies of sound, some growing louder, some fainter, waxing and waning amid the rumble

of milk wagons and infrequent cars. Shrill
cries they were when near—well-known cries
that conveyed many meanings to the ears of
those of the slumbering millions of the great
city who waked to hear them. Cries that
bore upon their significant, small volume the
weight of a world's woe and laughter and delight and stress. To some, cowering beneath
the protection of a night's ephemeral cover,
they brought news of the hideous, bright
day; to others, wrapped in happy sleep, they
announced a morning that would dawn blacker
than sable night. To many of the rich they
brought a besom to sweep away what had
been theirs while the stars shone; to the poor
they brought—another day.

All over the city the cries were starting up,
keen and sonorous, heralding the chances that
the slipping of one cogwheel in the machinery
of time had made; apportioning to the sleepers
while they lay at the mercy of fate, the vengeance, profit, grief, reward, and doom that
the new figure in the calendar had brought
them. Shrill and yet plaintive were the cries,
as if the young voices grieved that so much
evil and so little good was in their irresponsible hands. Thus echoed in the streets of

the helpless city the transmission of the latest
decrees of the gods, the cries of the newsboys—
the Clarion Call of the Press.

Woods flipped a dime to the waiter, and
said:

"Get me a *Morning Mars*."

When the paper came he glanced at its
first page, and then tore a leaf out of his
memorandum book and began to write on it
with the little gold pencil.

"What's the news?" yawned Kernan.

Woods flipped over to him the piece of
writing:

THE NEW YORK "MORNING MARS":
Please pay to the order of John Kernan the one
thousand dollars reward coming to me for his arrest
and conviction.

BARNARD WOODS.

"I kind of thought they would do that,"
said Woods, "when you were jollying 'em
so hard. Now, Johnny, you'll come to the
police station with me."

XXI

A RETRIEVED REFORMATION

A GUARD came to the prison shoe-shop, where Jimmy Valentine was assiduously stitching uppers, and escorted him to the front office. There the warden handed Jimmy his pardon, which had been signed that morning by the governor. Jimmy took it in a tired kind of way. He had served nearly ten months of a four-year sentence. He had expected to stay only about three months, at the longest. When a man with as many friends on the outside as Jimmy Valentine had is received in the "stir" it is hardly worth while to cut his hair.

"Now, Valentine," said the warden, "you'll go out in the morning. Brace up, and make a man of yourself. You're not a bad fellow at heart. Stop cracking safes, and live straight."

"Me?" said Jimmy, in surprise. "Why, I never cracked a safe in my life."

"Oh, no," laughed the warden. "Of course not. Let's see, now. How was it you happened to get sent up on that Springfield job? Was it because you wouldn't prove an alibi for fear of compromising somebody in extremely high-toned society? Or was it simply a case of a mean old jury that had it in for you? It's always one or the other with you innocent victims."

"Me?" said Jimmy, still blankly virtuous. "Why, warden, I never was in Springfield in my life!"

"Take him back, Cronin," smiled the warden, "and fix him up with outgoing clothes. Unlock him at seven in the morning, and let him come to the bull-pen. Better think over my advice, Valentine."

At a quarter past seven on the next morning Jimmy stood in the warden's outer office. He had on a suit of the villainously fitting, ready-made clothes and a pair of the stiff, squeaky shoes that the state furnishes to its discharged compulsory guests.

The clerk handed him a railroad ticket and the five-dollar bill with which the law expected him to rehabilitate himself into good citizenship and prosperity. The warden gave him a cigar, and shook hands. Valentine, 9762, was chronicled on the books "Pardoned by Governor," and Mr. James Valentine walked out into the sunshine.

Disregarding the song of the birds, the waving green trees, and the smell of the flowers, Jimmy headed straight for a restaurant. There he tasted the first sweet joys of liberty in the shape of a broiled chicken and a bottle of white wine—followed by a cigar a grade better than the one the warden had given him. From there he proceeded leisurely to the depot. He tossed a quarter into the hat of a blind man sitting by the door, and boarded his train. Three hours set him down in a little town near the state line. He went to the café of one Mike Dolan and shook hands with Mike, who was alone behind the bar.

"Sorry we couldn't make it sooner, Jimmy, me boy," said Mike. "But we had that protest from Springfield to buck against, and the governor nearly balked. Feeling all right?"

"Fine," said Jimmy. "Got my key?"

He got his key and went upstairs, unlocking the door of a room at the rear. Everything was just as he had left it. There on the floor was still Ben Price's collar-button that had been torn from that eminent detective's shirt-band when they had overpowered Jimmy to arrest him.

Pulling out from the wall a folding-bed, Jimmy slid back a panel in the wall and dragged out a dust-covered suit-case. He opened this and gazed fondly at the finest set of burglar's tools in the East. It was a complete set, made of specially tempered steel, the latest designs in drills, punches, braces, and bits, jimmies, clamps, and augers, with two or three novelties, invented by Jimmy himself, in which he took pride. Over nine hundred dollars they had cost him to have made at ——, a place where they make such things for the profession.

In half an hour Jimmy went downstairs and through the café. He was now dressed in tasteful and well-fitting clothes, and carried his dusted and cleaned suit-case in his hand.

"Got anything on?" asked Mike Dolan genially.

"Me?" said Jimmy, in a puzzled tone. "I don't understand. I'm representing the New York Amalgamated Short Snap Biscuit Cracker and Frazzled Wheat Company."

This statement delighted Mike to such an extent that Jimmy had to take a seltzer-and-milk on the spot. He never touched "hard" drinks.

A week after the release of Valentine, 9762, there was a neat job of safe-burglary done in Richmond, Indiana, with no clue to the author. A scant eight hundred dollars was all that was secured. Two weeks after that a patented, improved, burglar-proof safe in Logansport was opened like a cheese to the tune of fifteen hundred dollars, currency; securities and silver untouched. That began to interest the rogue-catchers. Then an old-fashioned bank-safe in Jefferson City became active and threw out of its crater an eruption of bank-notes amounting to five thousand dollars. The losses were now high enough to bring the matter up into Ben Price's class of work. By comparing notes, a remark-able similarity in the methods of the burglar-ies was noticed. Ben Price investigated the scenes of the robberies, and was heard to re-mark:

"That's Dandy Jim Valentine's auto-graph. He's resumed business. Look at that combination knob—jerked out as easy as

pulling up a radish in wet weather.   He's got
the only clamps that can do it.   And look
how clean those tumblers were punched out!
Jimmy never has to drill but one hole.   Yes,
I guess I want Mr. Valentine.   He'll do his
bit next time without any short-time or
clemency foolishness."

Ben Price knew Jimmy's habits.   He had
learned them while working up the Springfield case.   Long jumps, quick get-aways, no
confederates, and a taste for good society—
these ways had helped Mr. Valentine to become noted as a successful dodger of retribution.   It was given out that Ben Price had
taken up the trail of the elusive cracksman,
and other people with burglar-proof safes
felt more at ease.

One afternoon Jimmy Valentine and his
suit-case climbed out of the mail-hack in Elmore, a little town five miles off the railroad
down in the black-jack country of Arkansas.
Jimmy, looking like an athletic young senior
just home from college, went down the board
side-walk toward the hotel.

A young lady crossed the street, passed him
at the corner, and entered a door over which
was the sign "The Elmore Bank."   Jimmy

Valentine looked into her eyes, forgot what he was, and became another man. She lowered her eyes and coloured slightly. Young men of Jimmy's style and looks were scarce in Elmore.

Jimmy collared a boy that was loafing on the steps of the bank as if he were one of the stockholders, and began to ask him questions about the town, feeding him dimes at intervals. By and by the young lady came out, looking royally unconscious of the young man with the suit-case, and went her way.

"Isn't that young lady Miss Polly Simpson?" asked Jimmy, with specious guile.

"Naw," said the boy. "She's Annabel Adams. Her pa owns this bank. What'd you come to Elmore for? Is that a gold watch-chain? I'm going to get a bulldog. Got any more dimes?"

Jimmy went to the Planters' Hotel, registered as Ralph D. Spencer, and engaged a room. He leaned on the desk and declared his platform to the clerk. He said he had come to Elmore to look for a location to go into business. How was the shoe business, now, in the town? He had thought of the shoe business. Was there an opening?

The clerk was impressed by the clothes and manner of Jimmy. He, himself, was something of a pattern of fashion to the thinly gilded youth of Elmore, but he now perceived his shortcomings. While trying to figure out Jimmy's manner of tying his four-in-hand he cordially gave information.

Yes, there ought to be a good opening in the shoe line. There wasn't an exclusive shoe-store in the place. The dry-goods and general stores handled them. Business in all lines was fairly good. Hoped Mr. Spencer would decide to locate in Elmore. He would find it a pleasant town to live in, and the people very sociable.

Mr. Spencer thought he would stop over in the town a few days and look over the situation. No, the clerk needn't call the boy. He would carry up his suit-case, himself; it was rather heavy.

Mr. Ralph Spencer, the phœnix that arose from Jimmy Valentine's ashes—ashes left by the flame of a sudden and alterative attack of love—remained in Elmore, and prospered. He opened a shoe-store and secured a good run of trade.

Socially he was also a success, and made

many friends. And he accomplished the wish of his heart. He met Miss Annabel Adams, and became more and more captivated by her charms.

At the end of a year the situation of Mr. Ralph Spencer was this: he had won the respect of the community, his shoe-store was flourishing, and he and Annabel were engaged to be married in two weeks. Mr. Adams, the typical, plodding, country banker, approved of Spencer. Annabel's pride in him almost equalled her affection. He was as much at home in the family of Mr. Adams and that of Annabel's married sister as if he were already a member.

One day Jimmy sat down in his room and wrote this letter, which he mailed to the safe address of one of his old friends in St. Louis:

DEAR OLD PAL:

I want you to be at Sullivan's place, in Little Rock, next Wednesday night, at nine o'clock. I want you to wind up some little matters for me. And, also, want to make you a present of my kit of tools. I know you'll be glad to get them—you couldn't duplicate the lot for a thousand dollars. Say, Billy, I've quit the old business—a year ago. I've got a nice store. I'm making an honest living, and I'm going

to marry the finest girl on earth two weeks from now.
It's the only life, Billy—the straight one. I wouldn't
touch a dollar of another man's money now for a million. After I get married I'm going to sell out and go
West, where there won't be so much danger of having
old scores brought up against me. I tell you, Billy,
she's an angel. She believes in me; and I wouldn't
do another crooked thing for the whole world. Be
sure to be at Sully's, for I must see you. I'll bring
along the tools with me.

Your old friend,
JIMMY.

On the Monday night after Jimmy wrote
this letter, Ben Price jogged unobtrusively
into Elmore in a livery buggy. He lounged
about town in his quiet way until he found
out what he wanted to know. From the
drug-store across the street from Spencer's
shoe-store he got a good look at Ralph D.
Spencer.

"Going to marry the banker's daughter
are you, Jimmy?" said Ben to himself softly.
"Well, I don't know!"

The next morning Jimmy took breakfast
at the Adamses. He was going to Little
Rock that day to order his wedding-suit and
buy something nice for Annabel. That would
be the first time he had left town since he

came to Elmore. It had been more than a year now since those last professional "jobs," and he thought he could safely venture out.

After breakfast quite a family party went downtown together—Mr. Adams, Annabel, Jimmy, and Annabel's married sister with her two little girls, aged five and nine. They came by the hotel where Jimmy still boarded, and he ran up to his room and brought along his suit-case. Then they went on to the bank. There stood Jimmy's horse and buggy and Dolph Gibson, who was going to drive him over to the railroad station.

All went inside the high, carved oak railings into the banking-room—Jimmy included, for Mr. Adams's future son-in-law was welcome anywhere. The clerks were pleased to be greeted by the good-looking, agreeable young man who was going to marry Miss Annabel. Jimmy set his suit-case down. Annabel, whose heart was bubbling with happiness and lively youth, put on Jimmy's hat, and picked up the suit-case. "Wouldn't I make a nice drummer?" said Annabel. "My! Ralph, how heavy it is? Feels like it was full of gold bricks."

"Lot of nickel-plated shoe-horns in there,"

said Jimmy, coolly, "that I'm going to return. Thought I'd save express charges by taking them up. I'm getting awfully economical."

The Elmore Bank had just put in a new safe and vault. Mr. Adams was very proud of it, and insisted on an inspection by every one. The vault was a small one, but it had a new, patented door. It fastened with three solid steel bolts thrown simultaneously with a single handle, and had a time-lock. Mr. Adams beamingly explained its workings to Mr. Spencer, who showed a courteous but not too intelligent interest. The two children, May and Agatha, were delighted by the shining metal and funny clock and knobs.

While they were thus engaged Ben Price sauntered in and leaned on his elbow, looking casually inside between the railings. He told the teller that he didn't want anything; he was just waiting for a man he knew.

Suddenly there was a scream or two from the women, and a commotion. Unperceived by the elders, May, the nine-year-old girl, in a spirit of play, had shut Agatha in the vault. She had then shot the bolts and turned the knob of the combination as she had seen Mr. Adams do.

The old banker sprang to the handle and tugged at it for a moment. "The door can't be opened," he groaned. "The clock hasn't been wound nor the combination set."

Agatha's mother screamed again, hysterically.

"Hush!" said Mr. Adams, raising his trembling hand. "All be quiet for a moment. Agatha!" he called as loudly as he could. "Listen to me." During the following silence they could just hear the faint sound of the child wildly shrieking in the dark vault in a panic of terror.

"My precious darling!" wailed the mother. "She will die of fright! Open the door! Oh, break it open! Can't you men do something?"

"There isn't a man nearer than Little Rock who can open that door," said Mr. Adams, in a shaky voice. "My God! Spencer, what shall we do? That child—she can't stand it long in there. There isn't enough air, and, besides, she'll go into convulsions from fright."

Agatha's mother, frantic now, beat the door of the vault with her hands. Somebody wildly suggested dynamite. Annabel turned to Jimmy, her large eyes full of anguish, but

not yet despairing. To a woman nothing
seems quite impossible to the powers of the
man she worships.

"Can't you do something, Ralph—*try*,
won't you?"

He looked at her with a queer, soft smile on
his lips and in his keen eyes.

"Annabel," he said, "give me that rose you
are wearing, will you?"

Hardly believing that she heard him aright,
she unpinned the bud from the bosom of her
dress, and placed it in his hand.   Jimmy stuf-
fed it into his vest-pocket, threw off his coat,
and pulled up his shirt-sleeves. With that
act Ralph D. Spencer passed away and
Jimmy Valentine took his place.

"Get away from the door, all of you," he
commanded shortly.

He set his suit-case on the table, and opened
it out flat.   From that time on he seemed to
be unconscious of the presence of any one else.
He laid out the shining, queer implements
swiftly and orderly, whistling softly to himself as he always did when at work. In
a deep silence and immovable, the others
watched him as if under a spell.

In a minute Jimmy's pet drill was biting

smoothly into the steel door. In ten minutes—breaking his own burglarious record—
he threw back the bolts and opened the door.

Agatha, almost collapsed, but safe, was
gathered into her mother's arms.

Jimmy Valentine put on his coat, and
walked outside the railings toward the front
door. As he went he thought he heard a far-
away voice that he once knew call "Ralph!"
But he never hesitated.

At the door a big man stood somewhat in
his way.

"Hello, Ben!" said Jimmy, still with his
strange smile "Got around at last, have
you? Well, let's go. I don't know that it
makes much difference, now."

And then Ben Price acted rather strangely.

"Guess you're mistaken, Mr. Spencer," he
said. "Don't believe I recognize you. Your
buggy's waiting for you, ain't it?"

And Ben Price turned and strolled down
the street.

XXII

A DOUBLE-DYED DECEIVER

THE trouble began in Laredo. It was the Llano Kid's fault, for he should have confined his habit of manslaughter to Mexicans. But the Kid was past twenty; and to have only Mexicans to one's credit at twenty is to blush unseen on the Rio Grande border.

It happened in old Justo Valdos's gambling house. There was a poker game at which sat players who were not all friends, as happens often where men ride in from afar to shoot Folly as she gallops. There was a row over so small a matter as a pair of queens; and when the smoke had cleared away it was found that the Kid had committed an indiscretion, and his adversary had been guilty of a blunder. For, the unfortunate combatant, instead of being a Greaser, was a high-blooded youth from the cow ranches, of about the Kid's own age and possessed of friends and champions. His blunder in missing the Kid's

right ear only a sixteenth of an inch when he
pulled his gun did not lessen the indiscretion
of the better marksman.

The Kid, not being equipped with a ret-
inue, nor bountifully supplied with personal
admirers and supporters—on account of a
rather umbrageous reputation, even for the
border—considered it not incompatible with
his indisputable gameness to perform that
judicious tractional act known as "pulling
his freight."

Quickly the avengers gathered and sought
him. Three of them overtook him within
a rod of the station. The Kid turned and
showed his teeth in that brilliant but mirthless
smile that usually preceded his deeds of in-
solence and violence, and his pursuers fell
back without making it necessary for him
even to reach for his weapon.

But in this affair the Kid had not felt the
grim thirst for encounter that usually urged
him on to battle. It had been a purely
chance row, born of the cards and certain
epithets impossible for a gentleman to brook
that had passed between the two. The Kid
had rather liked the slim, haughty, brown-
faced young chap whom his bullet had cut

off in the first pride of manhood. And now he wanted no more blood. He wanted to get away and have a good long sleep somewhere in the sun on the mesquite grass with his handkerchief over his face. Even a Mexican might have crossed his path in safety while he was in this mood.

The Kid openly boarded the north-bound passenger train that departed five minutes later. But at Webb, a few miles out, where it was flagged to take on a traveller, he abandoned that manner of escape. There were telegraph stations ahead; and the Kid looked askance at electricity and steam. Saddle and spur were his rocks of safety.

The man whom he had shot was a stranger to him. But the Kid knew that he was of the Coralitos outfit from Hidalgo; and that the punchers from that ranch were more relentless and vengeful than Kentucky feudists when wrong or harm was done to one of them. So, with the wisdom that has characterized many great fighters, the Kid decided to pile up as many leagues as possible of chaparral and pear between himself and the retaliation of the Coralitos bunch.

Near the station was a store; and near the

store, scattered among the mesquites and elms, stood the saddle horses of the customers. Most of them waited, half asleep, with sagging limbs and drooping heads. But one, a long-legged roan with a curved neck, snorted and pawed the turf. Him the Kid mounted, gripped with his knees, and slapped gently with the owner's own quirt.

If the slaying of the temerarious cardplayer had cast a cloud over the Kid's standing as a good and true citizen, this last act of his veiled his figure in the darkest shadows of disrepute. On the Rio Grande border if you take a man's life you sometimes take trash; but if you take his horse, you take a thing the loss of which renders him poor, indeed, and which enriches you not—if you are caught. For the Kid there was no turning back now.

With the springing roan under him he felt little care or uneasiness. After a five-mile gallop he drew in to the plainsman's jogging trot, and rode northeastward toward the Nueces River bottoms. He knew the country well—its most tortuous and obscure trails through the great wilderness of brush and pear, and its camps and lonesome ranches where one might find safe entertainment. Always he bore to the east; for the Kid had never seen the ocean, and he had a fancy to lay his hand upon the mane of the great Gulf, the gamesome colt of the greater waters.

So after three days he stood on the shore at Corpus Christi, and looked out across the gentle ripples of a quiet sea.

Captain Boone, of the schooner *Flyaway*, stood near his skiff, which one of his crew was guarding in the surf. When ready to sail he had discovered that one of the necessaries of life, in the parallelogrammatic shape of plug tobacco, had been forgotten. A sailor had been dispatched for the missing cargo. Meanwhile the captain paced the sands, chewing profanely at his pocket store.

A slim, wiry youth in high-heeled boots came down to the water's edge. His face was boyish, but with a premature severity that hinted at a man's experience. His complexion was naturally dark; and the sun and wind of an outdoor life had burned it to a coffee brown. His hair was as black and straight as an Indian's; his face had not yet been upturned to the humiliation of a razor; his eyes were a cold and steady blue. He carried his left arm somewhat away from his body, for pearl-handled .45s are frowned upon by town mar-shals, and are a little bulky when packed in the left armhole of one's vest. He looked beyond Captain Boone at the gulf with the impersonal and expressionless dignity of a Chinese emperor.

"Thinkin' of buyin' that'ar gulf, buddy?" asked the captain, made sarcastic by his narrow escape from a tobaccoless voyage.

"Why, no," said the Kid gently, "I reckon not. I never saw it before. I was just looking at it. Not thinking of selling it, are you?"

"Not this trip," said the captain. "I'll send it to you C. O. D. when I get back to Buenas Tierras. Here comes that capstan-footed lubber with the chewin'. I ought to've weighed anchor an hour ago."

"Is that your ship out there?" asked the Kid.

"Why, yes," answered the captain, "if you want to call a schooner a ship, and I don't mind lyin'. But you better say Miller and Gonzales, owners, and ordinary plain, Billy-be-damned old Samuel K. Boone, skip-per."

"Where are you going to?" asked the refugee.

"Buenas Tierras, coast of South America— I forgot what they called the country the last time I was there. Cargo—lumber, corrugated iron, and machetes."

"What kind of a country is it?" asked the Kid—"hot or cold?"

"Warmish, buddy," said the captain. "But a regular Paradise Lost for elegance of scenery and be-yooty of geography. Ye're wakened every morning by the sweet singin' of red birds with seven purple tails, and the sighin' of breezes in the posies and roses. And the inhabitants never work, for they can reach out and pick steamer baskets of the choicest hothouse fruit without gettin' out of bed. And there's no Sunday and no ice and no rent and no troubles and no use and no nothin'. It's a great country for a man to go to sleep with, and wait for somethin' to turn up. The bananys and oranges and hurricanes and pineapples that ye eat comes from there."

"That sounds to me!" said the Kid, at last betraying interest. "What'll the expressage be to take me out there with you?"

"Twenty-four dollars," said Captain Boone; "grub and transportation. Second cabin. I haven't got a first cabin."

"You've got my company," said the Kid, pulling out a buckskin bag.

With three hundred dollars he had gone to Laredo for his regular "blowout." The duel in Valdos's had cut short his season of hilarity, but it had left him with nearly $200 for aid in the flight that it had made necessary.

"All right, buddy," said the captain. "I hope your ma won't blame me for this little childish escapade of yours." He beckoned to one of the boat's crew. "Let Sanchez lift you out to the skiff so you won't get your feet wet."

Thacker, the United States consul at Buenas Tierras, was not yet drunk. It was only eleven o'clock; and he never arrived at his desired state of beatitude—a state wherein he sang ancient maudlin vaudeville songs and pelted his screaming parrot with banana peels—until the middle of the afternoon. So, when he looked up from his hammock at the sound of a slight cough, and saw the Kid standing in the door of the consulate, he was still in a condition to extend the hospitality and courtesy due from the representative of a great nation. "Don't disturb yourself," said the Kid easily. "I just dropped in. They told me it was customary to light at your camp before starting in to round up the town. I just came in on a ship from Texas."

"Glad to see you, Mr.——," said the consul.

The Kid laughed.

"Sprague Dalton," he said. "It sounds funny to me to hear it. I'm called the Llano Kid in the Rio Grande country."

"I'm Thacker," said the consul. "Take that cane-bottom chair. Now if you've come to invest, you want somebody to advise you. These dingies will cheat you out of the gold in your teeth if you don't understand their ways. Try a cigar?"

"Much obliged," said the Kid, "but if it wasn't for my corn shucks and the little bag in my back pocket I couldn't live a minute." He took out his "makings," and rolled a cigarette.

"They speak Spanish here," said the consul. "You'll need an interpreter. If there's anything I can do, why, I'd be delighted. If you're buying fruit lands or looking for a concession of any sort, you'll want somebody who knows the ropes to look out for you."

"I speak Spanish," said the Kid, "about nine times better than I do English. Everybody speaks it on the range where I come from. And I'm not in the market for anything."

"You speak Spanish?" said Thacker thoughtfully. He regarded the Kid absorbedly.

"You look like a Spaniard, too," he continued. "And you're from Texas. And you can't be more than twenty or twenty-one. I wonder if you've got any nerve."

"You got a deal of some kind to put through?" asked the Texan, with unexpected shrewdness.

"Are you open to a proposition?" said Thacker.

"What's the use to deny it?" said the Kid. "I got into a little gun frolic down in Laredo and plugged a white man. There wasn't any Mexican handy. And I come down to your parrot-and-monkey range just for to smell the morning-glories and marigolds. Now, do you *sabe* ?"

Thacker got up and closed the door.

"Let me see your hand," he said.

He took the Kid's left hand, and examined the back of it closely.

"I can do it," he said excitedly. "Your flesh is as hard as wood and as healthy as a baby's. It will heal in a week."

"If it's a fist fight you want to back me for," said the Kid, "don't put your money up yet. Make it gun work, and I'll keep you company. But no barehanded scrapping, like ladies at a tea-party, for me."

"It's easier than that," said Thacker. "Just step here, will you?"

Through the window he pointed to a two-story white-stuccoed house with wide galleries rising amid the deep-green tropical foliage on a wooded hill that sloped gently from the sea.

"In that house," said Thacker, "a fine old Castilian gentleman and his wife are yearning to gather you into their arms and fill your pockets with money. Old Santos Urique lives there. He owns half the gold-mines in the country."

"You haven't been eating loco weed, have you?" asked the Kid.

"Sit down again," said Thacker, "and I'll

tell you. Twelve years ago they lost a kid.
No, he didn't die—although most of 'em here
do from drinking the surface water.   He was a
wild little devil, even if he wasn't but eight
years old.   Everybody knows about it.   Some
Americans who were through here prospecting
for gold had letters to Señor Urique, and the
boy was a favourite with them.   They filled
his head with big stories about the States;
and about a month after they left, the kid
disappeared, too.   He was supposed to have
stowed himself away among the banana
bunches on a fruit steamer, and gone to New
Orleans.   He was seen once afterward in
Texas, it was thought, but they never heard
anything more of him.   Old Urique has
spent thousands of dollars having him looked
for.   The madam was broken up worst of all.
The kid was her life.   She wears mourning
yet.   But they say she believes he'll come
back to her some day, and never gives up
hope.   On the back of the boy's left hand
was tattooed a flying eagle carrying a spear in
his claws.   That's old Urique's coat of arms
or something that he inherited in Spain."

The Kid raised his left hand slowly and
gazed at it curiously.

"That's it," said Thacker, reaching behind the official desk for his bottle of smuggled brandy. "You're not so slow. I can do it. What was I consul at Sandakan for? I never knew till now. In a week I'll have the eagle bird with the frog-sticker blended in so you'd think you were born with it. I brought a set of the needles and ink just because I was sure you'd drop in some day, Mr. Dalton."

"Oh, hell," said the Kid. "I thought I told you my name!"

"All right, 'Kid,' then. It won't be that long. How does Señorito Urique sound, for a change?"

"I never played son any that I remember of," said the Kid. "If I had any parents to mention they went over the divide about the time I gave my first bleat. What is the plan of your round-up?"

Thacker leaned back against the wall and held his glass up to the light.

"We've come now," said he, "to the question of how far you're willing to go in a little matter of the sort."

"I told you why I came down here," said the Kid simply.

"A good answer," said the Consul. "But

272 A Double–Dyed Deceiver

you won't have to go that far. Here's the
scheme. After I get the trademark tattooed
on your hand I'll notify old Urique. In the
meantime I'll furnish you with all of the
family history I can find out, so you can be
studying up points to talk about. You've
got the looks, you speak the Spanish, you know
the facts, you can tell about Texas, you've
got the tattoo mark. When I notify them
that the rightful heir has returned and is
waiting to know whether he will be received
and pardoned, what will happen? They'll
simply rush down here and fall on your neck,
and the curtain goes down for refreshments
and a stroll in the lobby."

"I'm waiting," said the Kid. "I haven't
had my saddle off in your camp long, pardner,
and I never met you before; but if you intend
to let it go at a parental blessing, why, I'm
mistaken in my man, that's all."

"Thanks," said the consul. "I haven't
met anybody in a long time that keeps up
with an argument as well as you 'do. The
rest of it is simple. If they take you in only
for a while it's long enough. Don't give 'em
time to hunt up the strawberry mark on your
left shoulder. Old Urique keeps anywhere

from $50,000 to $100,000 in his house all the
time in a little safe that you could open with a
shoe buttoner. Get it. My skill as a tat-
tooer is worth half the boodle. We go halves
and catch a tramp steamer for Rio Janeiro.
Let the United States go to pieces if it can't
get along without my services. *Que dice,
señor?*"

"It sounds to me!" said the Kid, nodding
his head. "I'm out for the dust."

"All right, then," said Thacker. "You'll
have to keep close until we get the bird on
you. You can live in the back room here.
I do my own cooking, and I'll make you as
comfortable as a parsimonious Government
will allow me."

Thacker had set the time at a week, but it
was two weeks before the design that he
patiently tattooed upon the Kid's hand was
to his notion. And then Thacker called a
muchacho, and dispatched this note to the
intended victim:

El Señor Don Santos Urique,
   La Casa Blanca,
My Dear Sir:
  I beg permission to inform you that there is in my
house as a temporary guest a young man who arrived

in Buenas Tierras from the United States some days
ago. Without wishing to excite any hopes that may
not be realized, I think there is a possibility of his
being your long-absent son. It might be well for you
to call and see him. If he is, it is my opinion that his
intention was to return to his home, but upon arriving
here, his courage failed him from doubts as to how
he would be received.

Your true servant,
THOMPSON THACKER.

Half an hour afterward—quick time for
Buenas Tierras—Señor Urique's ancient landau drove to the consul's door, with the
barefooted coachman beating and shouting
at the team of fat, awkward horses.

A tall man with a white moustache alighted,
and assisted to the ground a lady who was
dressed and veiled in unrelieved black.

The two hastened inside, and were met by
Thacker with his best diplomatic bow. By
his desk stood a slender young man with clear-
cut, sun-browned features and smoothly
brushed black hair.

Señora Urique threw back her heavy veil
with a quick gesture. She was past middle
age, and her hair was beginning to silver, but
her full, proud figure and clear olive skin

retained traces of the beauty peculiar to the Basque province. But, once you had seen her eyes, and comprehended the great sadness that was revealed in their deep shadows and hopeless expression, you saw that the woman lived only in some memory.

She bent upon the young man a long look of the most agonized questioning. Then her great black eyes turned, and her gaze rested upon his left hand. And then with a sob, not loud, but seeming to shake the room, she cried, "*Hijo mio !*" and caught the Llano Kid to her heart.

A month afterward the Kid came to the consulate in response to a message sent by Thacker.

He looked the young Spanish *caballero*. His clothes were imported, and the wiles of the jewellers had not been spent upon him in vain. A more than respectable diamond shone on his finger as he rolled a shuck cigarette.

"What's doing?" asked Thacker.

"Nothing much," said the Kid calmly. "I eat my first iguana steak to-day. They're them big lizards, you *sabe* ? I reckon, though,

that frijoles and side bacon would do me about
as well.   Do you care for iguanas, Thacker?"

"No, nor for some other kinds of reptiles,"
said Thacker.

It was three in the afternoon, and in another hour he would be in his state of beatitude.

"It's time you were making good, sonny,"
he went on, with an ugly look on his reddened
face.   "You're not playing up to me square.
You've been the prodigal son for four weeks
now, and you could have had veal for every
meal on a gold dish if you'd wanted it.   Now,
Mr. Kid, do you think it's right to leave me
out so long on a husk diet?   What's the
trouble?   Don't you get your filial eyes on
anything that looks like cash in the Casa
Blanca?   Don't tell me you don't.   Everybody knows where old Urique keeps his stuff.
It's U. S. currency, too; he don't accept anything else.   What's doing?   Don't say 'nothing' this time."

"Why, sure," said the Kid, admiring his
diamond, "there's plenty of money up there.
I'm no judge of collateral in bunches, but I
will undertake for to say that I've seen the
rise of $50,000 at a time in that tin grub

box that my adopted father calls his safe. And he lets me carry the key sometimes just to show me that he knows I'm the real little Francisco that strayed from the herd a long time ago."

"Well, what are you waiting for?" asked Thacker angrily. "Don't you forget that I can upset your apple-cart any day I want to. If old Urique knew you were an impostor, what sort of things would happen to you? Oh, you don't know this country, Mr. Texas Kid. The laws here have got mustard spread between 'em. These people here'd stretch you out like a frog that had been stepped on, and give you about fifty sticks at every corner of the plaza. And they'd wear every stick out, too. What was left of you they'd feed to alligators."

"I might as well tell you now, pardner," said the Kid, sliding down low on his steamer chair, "that things are going to stay just as they are. They're about right now."

"What do you mean?" asked Thacker, rattling the bottom of his glass on his desk.

"The scheme's off," said the Kid. "And whenever you have the pleasure of speaking to me address me as Don Francisco Urique.

I'll guarantee I'll answer to it. We'll let
Colonel Urique keep his money. His little
tin safe is as good as the time-locker in the
First National Bank of Laredo as far as you
and me are concerned."

"You're going to throw me down, then,
are you?" said the consul.

"Sure," said the Kid cheerfully. "Throw
you down. That's it. And now I'll tell you
why. The first night I was up at the Colonel's house they introduced me to a bedroom. No blankets on the floor—a real
room, with a bed and things in it. And before I was asleep, in comes this artificial
mother of mine and tucks in the covers.
'Panchito,' she says, 'my little lost one, God
has brought you back to me. I bless His
name forever.' It was that, or some truck
like that, she said. And down comes a drop
or two of rain and hits me on the nose. And
all that stuck by me, Mr. Thacker. And it's
been that way ever since. And it's got to
stay that way. Don't you think that it's
for what's in it for me, either, that I say so.
If you have any such ideas, keep 'em to
yourself. I haven't had much truck with
women in my life, and no mothers to speak

of, but here's a lady that we've got to keep fooled. Once she stood it; twice she won't. I'm a low-down wolf, and the devil may have sent me on this trail instead of God, but I'll travel it to the end. And now, don't forget that I'm Don Francisco Urique whenever you happen to mention my name."

"I'll expose you to-day, you—you double-dyed traitor," stammered Thacker.

The Kid arose and, without violence, took Thacker by the throat with a hand of steel, and shoved him slowly into a corner. Then he drew from under his left arm his pearl-handled .45 and poked the cold muzzle of it against the consul's mouth.

"I told you why I come here," he said, with his old freezing smile. "If I leave here, you'll be the reason. Never forget it, pardner. Now, what is my name?"

"Er—Don Francisco Urique," gasped Thacker.

From outside came a sound of wheels, and the shouting of some one, and the sharp thwacks of a wooden whipstock upon the backs of fat horses.

The Kid put up his gun, and walked toward the door. But he turned again and

came back to the trembling Thacker, and
held up his left hand with its back toward
the consul.

"There's one more reason," he said slowly,
"why things have got to stand as they are.
The fellow I killed in Laredo had one of them
same pictures on his left hand."

Outside, the ancient landau of Don Santos
Urique rattled to the door. The coachman
ceased his bellowing. Señora Urique, in a
voluminous gay gown of white lace and flying
ribbons, leaned forward with a happy look
in her great soft eyes.

"Are you within, dear son?" she called,
in the rippling Castilian.

"*Madre mia, yo vengo* [mother, I come],"
answered the young Don Francisco Urique.

XXIII

THE THEORY AND THE HOUND

Not many days ago my old friend from the tropics, J. P. Bridger, United States consul on the island of Ratona, was in the city. We had wassail and jubilee and saw the Flatiron building, and missed seeing the Bronxless menagerie by about a couple of nights. And then, at the ebb tide, we were walking up a street that parallels and parodies Broadway.

A woman with a comely and mundane countenance passed us, holding in leash a wheezing, vicious, waddling, brute of a yellow pug. The dog entangled himself with Bridger's legs and mumbled his ankles in a snarling, peevish, sulky bite. Bridger, with a happy smile, kicked the breath out of the brute; the woman showered us with a quick rain of well-conceived adjectives that left us in no doubt as to our place in her opinion, and we passed on. Ten yards farther an old woman with disordered white hair and her bankbook tucked well hidden beneath her tattered shawl begged. Bridger stopped and disinterred for her a quarter from his holiday waistcoat.

On the next corner a quarter of a ton of well-clothed man with a rice-powdered, fat, white jowl, stood holding the chain of a devil-born bulldog whose forelegs were strangers by the length of a dachshund. A little woman in a last season's hat confronted him and wept, which was plainly all she could do, while he cursed her in low, sweet, practised tones.

Bridger smiled again—strictly to himself—and this time he took out a little memorandum book and made a note of it. This he had no right to do without due explanation, and I said so.

"It's a new theory," said Bridger, "that I picked up down in Ratona. I've been gathering support for it as I knock about. The world isn't ripe for it yet, but—well, I'll tell you; and then you run your mind back along the people you've known and see what you make of it."

And so I cornered Bridger in a place where they have artificial palms and wine; and he

told me the story which is here in my words
and on his responsibility.

One afternoon at three o'clock, on the island of Ratona, a boy raced along the beach
screaming, "*Pajaro*, ahoy!"

Thus he made known the keenness of his
hearing and the justice of his discrimination
in pitch.

He who first heard and made oral proclama-
tion concerning the toot of an approaching
steamer's whistle, and correctly named the
steamer, was a small hero in Ratona—until
the next steamer came. Wherefore, there
was rivalry among the barefoot youth of
Ratona, and many fell victims to the softly
blown conch shells of sloops which, as they
enter harbour, sound surprisingly like a dis-
tant steamer's signal. And some could name
you the vessel when its call, in your duller
ears, sounded no louder than the sigh of the
wind through the branches of the cocoanut
palms.

But to-day he who proclaimed the *Pajaro*
gained his honours. Ratona bent its ear to
listen; and soon the deep-tongued blast grew
louder and nearer, and at length Ratona
saw above the line of palms on the low "point"

the two black funnels of the fruiter slowly creeping toward the mouth of the harbour.

You must know that Ratona is an island twenty miles off the south of a South American republic. It is a port of that republic; and it sleeps sweetly in a smiling sea, toiling not nor spinning; fed by the abundant tropics where all things "ripen, cease, and fall toward the grave."

Eight hundred people dream life away in a green-embowered village that follows the horseshoe curve of its bijou harbour. They are mostly Spanish and Indian mestizos, with a shading of San Domingo Negroes, a lightening of pure-blood Spanish officials, and a slight leavening of the froth of three or four pioneering white races. No steamers touch at Ratona save the fruit steamers which take on their banana inspectors there on their way to the coast. They leave Sunday newspapers, ice, quinine, bacon, watermelons, and vaccine matter at the island and that is about all the touch Ratona gets with the world.

The *Pajaro* paused at the mouth of the harbour, rolling heavily in the swell that sent the whitecaps racing beyond the smooth water inside. Already two dories from the village—one conveying fruit inspectors, the other going for what it could get—were half-way out to the steamer.

The inspector's dory was taken on board with them, and the *Pajaro* steamed away for the mainland for its load of fruit.

The other boat returned to Ratona bearing a contribution from the *Pajaro's* store of ice, the usual roll of newspapers and one passenger—Taylor Plunkett, sheriff of Chatham County, Kentucky.

Bridger, the United States consul at Ratona, was cleaning his rifle in the official shanty under a bread-fruit tree twenty yards from the water of the harbour. The consul occupied a place somewhat near the tail of his political party's procession. The music of the band wagon sounded very faintly to him in the distance. The plums of office went to others. Bridger's share of the spoils —the consulship at Ratona—was little more than a prune—a dried prune from the boarding-house department of the public crib. But $900 yearly was opulence in Ratona. Besides, Bridger had contracted a passion for shooting alligators in the lagoons near his consulate, and he was not unhappy.

He looked up from a careful inspection of his rifle lock and saw a broad man filling his doorway. A broad, noiseless, slow-moving man, sunburned almost to the brown of Van-dyke. A man of forty-five, neatly clothed in homespun, with scanty light hair, a close-clipped brown-and-gray beard, and pale-blue eyes expressing mildness and simplicity.

"You are Mr. Bridger, the consul," said the broad man. "They directed me here. Can you tell me what those big bunches of things like gourds are in those trees that look like feather dusters along the edge of the water?"

"Take that chair," said the consul, re-oiling his cleaning rag. "No, the other one —that bamboo thing won't hold you. Why, they're cocoanuts—green cocoanuts. The shell of 'em is always a light green before they're ripe."

"Much obliged," said the other man, sitting down carefully. "I didn't quite like to tell the folks at home they were olives unless I was sure about it. My name is Plunkett. I'm sheriff of Chatham County, Kentucky. I've got extradition papers in my pocket authorizing the arrest of a man on this is-

land. They've been signed by the President
of this country, and they're in correct shape.
The man's name is Wade Williams. He's in
the cocoanut raising business. What he's
wanted for is the murder of his wife two
years ago. Where can I find him?"

The consul squinted an eye and looked
through his rifle barrel.

"There's nobody on the island who calls
himself 'Williams,'" he remarked.

"Didn't suppose there was," said Plunkett
mildly. "He'll do by any other name."

"Besides myself," said Bridger, "there are
only two Americans on Ratona—Bob Reeves
and Henry Morgan."

"The man I want sells cocoanuts," suggested Plunkett.

"You see that cocoanut walk extending up
to the point?" said the consul, waving his
hand toward the open door. "That belongs
to Bob Reeves. Henry Morgan owns half
the trees to loo'ard on the island."

"One month ago," said the sheriff, "Wade
Williams wrote a confidential letter to a
man in Chatham County, telling him where
he was and how he was getting along. The
letter was lost; and the person that found it

gave it away. They sent me after him, and I've got the papers. I reckon he's one of your cocoanut men for certain."

"You've got his picture, of course," said Bridger. "It might be Reeves or Morgan, but I'd hate to think it. They're both as fine fellows as you'd meet in an all-day auto ride."

"No," doubtfully answered Plunkett; "there wasn't any picture of Williams to be had. And I never saw him myself. I've been sheriff only a year. But I've got a pretty accurate description of him. About 5 feet 11; dark hair and eyes; nose inclined to be Roman; heavy about the shoulders; strong, white teeth, with none missing; laughs a good deal, talkative; drinks considerably but never to intoxication; looks you square in the eye when talking; age thirty-five. Which one of your men does that description fit?"

The consul grinned broadly.

"I'll tell you what you do," he said, laying down his rifle and slipping on his dingy black alpaca coat. "You come along, Mr. Plunkett, and I'll take you up to see the boys. If you can tell which one of 'em your description fits better than it does the other you have the advantage of me."

Bridger conducted the sheriff out and along the hard beach close to which the tiny houses of the village were distributed. Immediately back of the town rose sudden, small, thickly wooded hills. Up one of these, by means of steps cut in the hard clay, the consul led Plunkett. On the very verge of an eminence was perched a two-room wooden cottage with a thatched roof. A Carib woman was washing clothes outside. The consul ushered the sheriff to the door of the room that overlooked the harbour.

Two men were in the room, about to sit down, in their shirt sleeves, to a table spread for dinner. They bore little resemblance one to the other in detail; but the general description given by Plunkett could have been justly applied to either. In height, colour of hair, shape of nose, build, and manners each of them tallied with it. They were fair types of jovial, ready-witted, broad-gauged Americans who had gravitated together for companionship in an alien land.

"Hello, Bridger!" they called in unison at sight of the consul. "Come and have dinner

with us!" And then they noticed Plunkett
at his heels, and came forward with hospitable
curiosity.

"Gentlemen," said the consul, his voice
taking on unaccustomed formality, "this is
Mr. Plunkett. Mr. Plunkett—Mr. Reeves
and Mr. Morgan."

The cocoanut barons greeted the newcomer
joyously. Reeves seemed about an inch taller
than Morgan, but his laugh was not quite as
loud. Morgan's eyes were deep brown;
Reeves's were black. Reeves was the host
and busied himself with fetching other chairs
and calling to the Carib woman for supple-
mental table ware. It was explained that
Morgan lived in a bamboo shack to "loo'ard,"
but that every day the two friends dined
together. Plunkett stood still during the
preparations, looking about mildly with his
pale-blue eyes. Bridger looked apologetic
and uneasy.

At length two other covers were laid and
the company was assigned to places. Reeves
and Morgan stood side by side across the
table from the visitors. Reeves nodded genially as a signal for all to seat themselves. And
then suddenly Plunkett raised his hand with a

gesture of authority.   He was looking straight
between Reeves and Morgan.

"Wade Williams," he said quietly, "you
are under arrest for murder."

Reeves and Morgan instantly exchanged a
quick, bright glance, the quality of which
was interrogation, with a seasoning of surprise.   Then, simultaneously they turned to
the speaker with a puzzled and frank depre-
cation in their gaze.

"Can't say that we understand you, Mr.
Plunkett," said Morgan cheerfully.   "Did
you say 'Williams'?"

"What's the joke, Bridgy?" asked Reeves,
turning to the consul with a smile.

Before Bridger could answer Plunkett spoke
again.

"I'll explain," he said quietly.   "One of
you don't need any explanation, but this is
for the other one.   One of you is Wade Williams of Chatham County, Kentucky.   You
murdered your wife on May 5th, two years
ago, after ill-treating and abusing her con-
tinually for five years.   I have the proper
papers in my pocket for taking you back
with me, and you are going.   We will return
on the fruit steamer that comes back by this

island to-morrow to leave its inspectors. I acknowledge, gentlemen, that I'm not quite sure which one of you is Williams. But Wade Williams goes back to Chatham County to-morrow. I want you to understand that."

A great sound of merry laughter from Morgan and Reeves went out over the still harbour. Two or three fishermen in the fleet of sloops anchored there looked up at the house of the diablos Americanos on the hill and wondered.

"My dear Mr. Plunkett," cried Morgan, conquering his mirth, "the dinner is getting cold. Let us sit down and eat. I am anxious to get my spoon into that sharkfin soup. Business afterward."

"Sit down, gentlemen, if you please," added Reeves pleasantly. "I am sure Mr. Plunkett will not object. Perhaps a little time may be of advantage to him in identifying— the gentleman he wishes to arrest."

"No objections, I'm sure," said Plunkett, dropping into his chair heavily. "I'm hungry myself. I didn't want to accept the hospitality of you folks without giving you notice; that's all."

Reeves set bottles and glasses on the table.

"There's cognac," he said, "and anisada, and Scotch 'smoke,' and rye. Take your choice."

Bridger chose rye, Reeves poured three fingers of Scotch for himself, Morgan took the same. The sheriff, against much protestation, filled his glass from the water bottle.

"Here's to the appetite," said Reeves, raising his glass, "of Mr. Williams!" Morgan's laugh and his drink encountering sent him into a choking splutter. All began to pay attention to the dinner, which was well cooked and palatable.

"Williams!" called Plunkett, suddenly and sharply.

All looked up wonderingly. Reeves found the sheriff's mild eye resting upon him. He flushed a little.

"See here," he said, with some asperity, "my name's Reeves, and I don't want you to——" But the comedy of the thing came to his rescue, and he ended with a laugh.

"I suppose, Mr. Plunkett," said Morgan, carefully seasoning an alligator pear, "that you are aware of the fact that you will import a good deal of trouble for yourself into Kentucky if you take back the wrong man—that is, of course, if you take anybody back?"

"Thank you for the salt," said the sheriff. "Oh, I'll take somebody back. It'll be one of you two gentlemen. Yes, I know I'd get stuck for damages if I make a mistake. But I'm going to try to get the right man."

"I'll tell you what you do," said Morgan, leaning forward with a jolly twinkle in his eyes. "You take me. I'll go without any trouble. The cocoanut business hasn't panned out well this year, and I'd like to make some extra money out of your bondsmen."

"That's not fair," chimed in Reeves. "I got only $16 a thousand for my last shipment. Take me, Mr. Plunkett."

"I'll take Wade Williams," said the sheriff, patiently, "or I'll come pretty close to it."

"It's like dining with a ghost," remarked Morgan, with a pretended shiver. "The ghost of a murderer, too! Will somebody pass the toothpicks to the shade of the haughty Mr. Williams?"

Plunkett seemed as unconcerned as if he were dining at his own table in Chatham County. He was a gallant trencherman, and the strange tropic viands tickled his palate. Heavy, commonplace, almost slothful in his movements, he appeared to be devoid of all the cunning and watchfulness of the sleuth. He even ceased to observe, with any sharpness or attempted discrimination, the two men, one of whom he had undertaken, with surprising self-confidence, to drag away upon the serious charge of wife-murder. Here, indeed, was a problem set before him that if wrongly solved would have amounted to his serious discomfiture, yet there he sat puzzling his soul (to all appearances) over the novel flavour of a broiled iguana cutlet.

The consul felt a decided discomfort. Reeves and Morgan were his friends and pals; yet the sheriff from Kentucky had a certain right to his official aid and moral support. So Bridger sat the silentest around the board and tried to estimate the peculiar situation. His conclusion was that both Reeves and Morgan, quickwitted, as he knew them to be, had conceived at the moment of Plunkett's disclosure of his mission—and in the brief space of a lightning flash—the idea that the other might be the guilty Williams; and that each of them had decided in that moment loyally to protect his comrade against the doom that threatened him. This was the consul's theory and if he had been a book-maker at a race of wits for life and liberty he would have offered heavy odds against the plodding sheriff from Chatham County, Kentucky.

When the meal was concluded the Carib woman came and removed the dishes and cloth. Reeves strewed the table with excellent cigars, and Plunkett, with the others, lighted one of these with evident gratification.

"I may be dull," said Morgan, with a grin and a wink at Bridger; "but I want to know if I am. Now, I say this is all a joke of Mr. Plunkett's, concocted to frighten two babes-in-th'e-woods. Is this Williamson to be taken seriously or not?"

"'Williams,'" corrected Plunkett gravely. "I never got off any jokes in my life. I know I wouldn't travel 2,000 miles to get off a poor one as this would be if I didn't take Wade Williams back with me. Gentlemen!" continued the sheriff, now letting his mild eyes travel impartially from one of the company to another, "see if you can find any joke in this case. Wade Williams is listening

to the words I utter now; but out of politeness I will speak of him as a third person.
For five years he made his wife lead the life
of a dog—No; I'll take that back. No dog
in Kentucky was ever treated as she was.
He spent the money that she brought him—
spent it at races, at the card table, and on
horses and hunting. He was a good fellow
to his friends, but a cold, sullen demon at
home. He wound up the five years of neg-
lect by striking her with his closed hand—a
hand as hard as a stone—when she was ill
and weak from suffering. She died the next
day; and he skipped. That's all there is to
it. It's enough. I never saw Williams; but
I knew his wife. I'm not a man to tell half.
She and I were keeping company when she
met him. She went to Louisville on a visit
and saw him there. I'll admit that he spoilt
my chances in no time. I lived then on the
edge of the Cumberland mountains. I was
elected sheriff of Chatham County a year
after Wade Williams killed his wife. My
official duty sends me out here after him;
but I'll admit that there's personal feeling,
too. And he's going back with me. Mr.—
er—Reeves, will you pass me a match?"

"Awfully imprudent of Williams," said Morgan, putting his feet up against the wall, "to strike a Kentucky lady. Seems to me I've heard they were scrappers."

"Bad, bad Williams," said Reeves, pouring out more "Scotch."

The two men spoke lightly, but the consul saw and felt the tension and the carefulness in their actions and words. "Good old fellows," he said to himself; "they're both all right. Each of 'em is standing by the other like a little brick church."

And then a dog walked into the room where they sat—a black-and-tan hound, long-eared, lazy, confident of welcome.

Plunkett turned his head and looked at the animal, which halted, confidently, within a few feet of his chair.

Suddenly the sheriff, with a deep-mouthed oath, left his seat and bestowed upon the dog a vicious and heavy kick, with his ponderous shoe.

The hound, heart-broken, astonished, with flapping ears and incurved tail, uttered a piercing yelp of pain and surprise.

Reeves and the consul remained in their chairs, saying nothing, but astonished at the

unexpected show of intolerance from the
easy-going man from Chatham County.

But Morgan, with a suddenly purpling
face, leaped to his feet and raised a threatening arm above the guest.

"You—brute!" he shouted passionately;
"why did you do that?"

Quickly the amenities returned, Plunkett
muttered some indistinct apology and re-
gained his seat. Morgan with a decided
effort controlled his indignation and also
returned to his chair.

And then Plunkett, with the spring of a tiger,
leaped around the corner of the table and snapped handcuffs on the paralyzed Morgan's wrists.

"Hound-lover and woman-killer!" he cried,
"get ready to meet your God."

When Bridger had finished I asked him:

"Did he get the right man?"

"He did," said the consul.

"And how did he know?" I inquired, being
in a kind of bewilderment.

"When he put Morgan in the dory," answered Bridger, "the next day to take him
aboard the *Pajaro*, this man Plunkett stopped
to shake hands with me and I asked him the
same question.

"'Mr. Bridger,' said he, 'I'm a Kentuckian, and I've seen a great deal of both men and animals. And I never yet saw a man that was overfond of horses and dogs but what was cruel to women.'"

XXIV

A BLACKJACK BARGAINER

THE most disreputable thing in Yancey Goree's law office was Goree himself, sprawled in his creaky old armchair. The rickety little office, built of red brick, was set flush with the street—the main street of the town of Bethel.

Bethel rested upon the foothills of the Blue Ridge. Above it the mountains were piled to the sky. Far below it the turbid Catawba gleamed yellow along its disconsolate valley.

The June day was at its sultriest hour. Bethel dozed in the tepid shade. Trade was not. It was so still that Goree, reclining in his chair, distinctly heard the clicking of the chips in the grand jury room, where the "courthouse gang" was playing poker. From the open back door of the office a well-worn path meandered across the grassy lot to the courthouse. The treading out of that path had cost Goree all he ever had—first inheritance of a few thousand dollars, next the old family home, and latterly the last shreds of his self-respect and manhood. The "gang" had cleaned him out. The broken gambler had turned drunkard and parasite; he had lived to see this day come when the men who had stripped him denied him a seat at the game. His word was no longer to be taken. The daily bouts at cards had arranged itself accordingly, and to him was assigned the ignoble part of the onlooker. The sheriff, the county clerk, a sportive deputy, a gay attorney, and a chalk-faced man hailing "from the valley," sat at table, and the sheared one was thus tacitly advised to go and grow more wool.

Soon wearying of his ostracism, Goree had departed for his office, muttering to himself as he unsteadily traversed the unlucky pathway. After a drink of corn whiskey from a demijohn under the table, he had flung himself into the chair, staring, in a sort of maudlin apathy, out at the mountains immersed in the summer haze. The little white patch he saw away up on the side of Blackjack was Laurel, the village near which he had been born and bred. There, also, was the birth-

place of the feud between the Gorees and the
Coltranes. Now no direct heir of the Gorees
survived except this plucked and singed bird
of misfortune. To the Coltranes, also, but
one male supporter was left—Colonel Abner
Coltrane, a man of substance and standing, a
member of the State Legislature, and a con-
temporary with Goree's father. The feud
had been a typical one of the region; it had
left a red record of hate, wrong, and slaughter.

But Yancey Goree was not thinking of
feuds. His befuddled brain was hopelessly
attacking the problem of the future mainte-
nance of himself and his favourite follies. Of
late, old friends of the family had seen to it
that he had whereof to eat and a place to sleep,
but whiskey they would not buy for him,
and he must have whiskey. His law business
was extinct; no case had been intrusted to
him in two years. He had been a borrower
and a sponge, and it seemed that if he fell
no lower it would be from lack of opportunity.
One more chance—he was saying to himself—
if he had one more stake at the game, he
thought he could win; but he had nothing
left to sell, and his credit was more than exhausted.

He could not help smiling, even in his misery, as he thought of the man to whom, six months before, he had sold the old Goree homestead. There had come from "back yan'" in the mountains two of the strangest creatures, a man named Pike Garvey and his wife. "Back yan'," with a wave of the hand toward the hills, was understood among the mountaineers to designate the remotest fastnesses, the unplumbed gorges, the haunts of lawbreakers, the wolf's den, and the boudoir of the bear. In the cabin far up on Blackjack's shoulder, in the wildest part of these retreats, this odd couple had lived for twenty years. They had neither dog nor children to mitigate the heavy silence of the hills. Pike Garvey was little known in the settlements, but all who had dealt with him pronounced him "crazy as a loon." He acknowledged no occupation save that of a squirrel hunter, but he "moonshined" occasionally by way of diversion. Once the "revenues" had dragged him from his lair, fighting silently and desperately like a terrier, and he had been sent to state's prison for two years. Released, he popped back into his hole like an angry weasel.

Fortune, passing over many anxious wooers, made a freakish flight into Blackjack's bosky pockets to smile upon Pike and his faithful partner.

One day a party of spectacled, knickerbockered, and altogether absurd prospectors invaded the vicinity of the Garvey's cabin. Pike lifted his squirrel rifle off the hooks and took a shot at them at long range on the chance of their being revenues. Happily he missed, and the unconscious agents of good luck drew nearer, disclosing their innocence of anything resembling law or justice. Later on, they offered the Garveys an enormous quantity of ready, green, crisp money for their thirty-acre patch of cleared land, mentioning, as an excuse for such a mad action, some irrelevant and inadequate nonsense about a bed of mica underlying the said property.

When the Garveys became possessed of so many dollars that they faltered in computing them, the deficiencies of life on Blackjack began to grow prominent. Pike began to talk of new shoes, a hogshead of tobacco to set in the corner, a new lock to his rifle; and, leading Martella to a certain spot on the

mountain-side, he pointed out to her how a
small cannon—doubtless a thing not beyond
the scope of their fortune in price—might be
planted so as to command and defend the sole
accessible trail to the cabin, to the confusion
of revenues and meddling strangers forever.

But Adam reckoned without his Eve. These
things represented to him the applied power
of wealth, but there slumbered in his dingy
cabin an ambition that soared far above his
primitive wants. Somewhere in Mrs. Garvey's bosom still survived a spot of femininity
unstarved by twenty years of Blackjack. For
so long a time the sounds in her ears had been
the scaly-barks dropping in the woods at
noon, and the wolves singing among the rocks
at night, and it was enough to have purged
her of vanities. She had grown fat and sad
and yellow and dull. But when the means
came, she felt a rekindled desire to assume
the perquisites of her sex—to sit at tea tables;
to buy inutile things; to whitewash the hideous veracity of life with a little form and
ceremony. So she coldly vetoed Pike's proposed system of fortifications, and announced
that they would descend upon the world, and
gyrate socially.

And thus, at length, it was decided, and the thing done. The village of Laurel was their compromise between Mrs. Garvey's preference for one of the large valley towns and Pike's hankering for primeval solitudes. Laurel yielded a halting round of feeble social distractions comportable with Martella's ambitions, and was not entirely without recommendation to Pike, its contiguity to the mountains presenting advantages for sudden retreat in case fashionable society should make it advisable.

Their descent upon Laurel had been coincident with Yancey Goree's feverish desire to convert property into cash, and they bought the old Goree homestead, paying four thousand dollars ready money into the spendthrift's shaking hands.

Thus it happened that while the disreputable last of the Gorees sprawled in his disreputable office, at the end of his row, spurned by the cronies whom he had gorged, strangers dwelt in the halls of his fathers.

A cloud of dust was rolling slowly up the parched street, with something travelling in the midst of it. A little breeze wafted the cloud to one side, and a new, brightly painted carryall, drawn by a slothful gray horse, became visible. The vehicle deflected from the middle of the street as it neared Goree's office, and stopped in the gutter directly in front of his door.

On the front seat sat a gaunt, tall man, dressed in black broadcloth, his rigid hands incarcerated in yellow kid gloves. On the back seat was a lady who triumphed over the June heat. Her stout form was armoured in a skin-tight silk dress of the description known as "changeable," being a gorgeous combination of shifting hues. She sat erect, waving a much-ornamented fan, with her eyes fixed stonily far down the street. However Martella Garvey's heart might be rejoicing at the pleasures of her new life, Blackjack had done his work with her exterior. He had carved her countenance to the image of emptiness and inanity; had imbued her with the stolidity of his crags and the reserve of his hushed interiors. She always seemed to hear, whatever her surroundings were, the scaly-barks falling and pattering down the mountainside. She could always hear the awful silence of Blackjack sounding through the stillest of nights.

Goree watched this solemn equipage, as it drove to his door, with only faint interest; but when the lank driver wrapped the reins about his whip, awkwardly descended, and stepped into the office, he rose unsteadily to receive him, recognizing Pike Garvey, the new, the transformed, the recently civilized.

The mountaineer took the chair Goree offered him. They who cast doubts upon Garvey's soundness of mind had a strong witness in the man's countenance. His face was too long, a dull saffron in hue, and immobile as a statue's. Pale-blue, unwinking round eyes without lashes added to the singularity of his gruesome visage. Goree was at a loss to account for the visit.

"Everything all right at Laurel, Mr. Garvey?" he inquired.

"Everything all right, sir, and mighty pleased is Missis Garvey and me with the property. Missis Garvey likes yo' old place, and she likes the neighbourhood. Society is what she 'lows she wants, and she is gettin' of it. The Rogerses, the Hapgoods, the Pratts, and the Troys hev been to see Missis Garvey, and she hev et meals to most of thar houses. The best folks hev axed her to differ'nt

kinds of doin's. I cyan't say, Mr. Goree,
that sech things suits me—fur me, give me
them thar." Garvey's huge, yellow-gloved
hand flourished in the direction of the mountains. "That's whar I b'long, 'mongst the
wild honey bees and the b'ars. But that
ain't what I come fur to say, Mr. Goree.
Thar's somethin' you got what me and Missis
Garvey wants to buy."

"Buy!" echoed Goree. "From me?" Then
he laughed harshly. "I reckon you are mistaken about that. I reckon you are mistaken
about that. I sold out to you, as you yourself expressed it, 'lock, stock, and barrel.'
There isn't even a ramrod left to sell."

"You've got it; and we 'uns want it. 'Take
the money,' says Missis Garvey, 'and buy it
fa'r and squar'.'"

Goree shook his head. "The cupboard's
bare," he said.

"We've riz," pursued the mountaineer, un-
deflected from his object, "a heap. We was
pore as possums, and now we could hev folks
to dinner every day. We been reco'nized,
Missis Garvey says, by the best society. But
there's somethin' we need we ain't got. She
says it ought to been put in the 'ventory

ov the sale, but it tain't thar. 'Take the money, then,' says she, 'and buy it fa'r and squar'.'"

"Out with it," said Goree, his racked nerves growing impatient.

Garvey threw his slouch hat upon the table, and leaned forward, fixing his unblinking eyes upon Goree's.

"There's a old feud," he said distinctly and slowly, " 'tween you 'uns and the Coltranes."

Goree frowned ominously. To speak of his feud to a feudist is a serious breach of the mountain etiquette. The man from "back yan'" knew it as well as the lawyer did.

"Na offense," he went on, "but purely in the way of business. Missis Garvey hev studied all about feuds. Most of the quality folks in the mountains hev 'em. The Settles and the Goforths, the Rankins and the Boyds, the Silers and the Galloways, hev all been cyarin' on feuds f'om twenty to a hundred year. The last man to drap was when yo' uncle, Jedge Paisley Goree, 'journed co't and shot Len Coltrane f'om the bench. Missis Garvey and me, we come f'om the po' white trash. Nobody wouldn't pick a feud with we 'uns, no mo'n with a fam'ly of treetoads.

Quality people everywhar, says Missis Garvey, has feuds. We 'uns ain't quality, but
we're buyin' into it as fur as we can. 'Take
the money, then,' says Missis Garvey, 'and
buy Mr. Goree's feud, fa'r and squar'.'"

The squirrel hunter straightened a leg half
across the room, drew a roll of bills from his
pocket, and threw them on the table.

"Thar's two hundred dollars, Mr. Goree;
what you would call a fa'r price for a feud
that's been 'lowed to run down like yourn
hev. Thar's only you left to cyar' on yo'
side of it, and you'd make mighty po' killin'.
I'll take it off yo' hands, and it'll set me and
Missis Garvey up among the quality. Thar's
the money."

The little roll of currency on the table
slowly untwisted itself, writhing and jumping
as its folds relaxed. In the silence that followed Garvey's last speech the rattling of
the poker chips in the court-house could be
plainly heard. Goree knew that the sheriff
had just won a pot, for the subdued whoop
with which he always greeted a victory floated
across the square upon the crinkly heat waves.
Beads of moisture stood on Goree's brow.
Stooping, he drew the wicker-covered demi-

John from under the table, and filled a tumbler from it.

"A little corn liquor, Mr. Garvey? Of course you are joking about—what you spoke of? Opens quite a new market, doesn't it? Feuds, prime, two-fifty to three. Feuds, slightly damaged—two hundred, I believe you said, Mr. Garvey?"

Goree laughed self-consciously.

The mountaineer took the glass Goree handed him, and drank the whiskey without a tremour of the lids of his staring eyes. The lawyer applauded the feat by a look of envious admiration. He poured his own drink, and took it like a drunkard, by gulps, and with shudders at the smell and taste.

"Two hundred," repeated Garvey. "Thar's the money."

A sudden passion flared up in Goree's brain. He struck the table with his fist. One of the bills flipped over and touched his hand. He flinched as if something had stung him.

"Do you come to me," he shouted, "seriously with such a ridiculous, insulting, darned fool proposition?"

"It's fa'r and squar'," said the squirrel hunter, but he reached out his hand as if to

take back the money; and then Goree knew
that his own flurry of rage had not been
from pride or resentment, but from anger at
himself, knowing that he would set foot in the
deeper depths that were being opened to him.
He turned in an instant from an outraged
gentleman to an anxious chafferer recom-
mending his goods.

"Don't be in a hurry, Garvey," he said, his
face crimson and his speech thick. "I accept your p-p-proposition, though it's dirt
cheap at two hundred. A t-trade's all right
when both p-purchaser and b-buyer are s-satis-
fied. Shall I w-wrap it up for you, Mr.
Garvey?"

Garvey rose, and shook out his broadcloth.
"Missis Garvey will be pleased. You air out
of it, and it stands Coltrane and Garvey. Just
a scrap ov writin', Mr. Goree, you bein' a
lawyer, to show we traded."

Goree seized a sheet of paper and a pen.
The money was clutched in his moist hand.
Everything else suddenly seemed to grow
trivial and light.

"Bill of sale, by all means. 'Right, title,
and interest in and to' . . . 'forever war-
rant and——' No, Garvey, we'll have to

leave out that 'defend,'" said Goree with a
loud laugh. "You'll have to defend this title
yourself."

The mountaineer received the amazing
screed that the lawyer handed him, folded it
with immense labour, and placed it carefully
in his pocket.

Goree was standing near the window. "Step
here," he said, raising his finger, "and I'll
show you your recently purchased enemy.
There he goes, down the other side of the
street."

The mountaineer crooked his long frame to
look through the window in the direction indicated by the other. Colonel Abner Coltrane, an erect, portly gentleman of about
fifty, wearing the inevitable long, double-
breasted frock coat of the Southern lawmaker,
and an old high silk hat, was passing on the
opposite sidewalk. As Garvey looked, Goree
glanced at his face. If there be such a thing
as a yellow wolf, here was its counterpart.
Garvey snarled as his unhuman eyes followed
the moving figure, disclosing long, amber-
coloured fangs.

"Is that him? Why, that's the man who
sent me to the pen'tentiary once!"

"He used to be district attorney," said Goree carelessly. "And, by the way, he's a first-class shot."

"I kin hit a squirrel's eye at a hundred yard," said Garvey. "So that thar's Coltrane! I made a better trade than I was thinkin'. I'll take keer ov this feud, Mr. Goree, better'n you ever did!"

He moved toward the door, but lingered there, betraying a slight perplexity.

"Anything else to-day?" inquired Goree with frothy sarcasm. "Any family traditions, ancestral ghosts, or skeletons in the closet? Prices as low as the lowest."

"Thar was another thing," replied the unmoved squirrel hunter, "that Missis Garvey was thinkin' of. 'Tain't so much in my line as t'other, but she wanted partic'lar that I should inquire, and ef you was willin', 'pay fur it,' she says, 'fa'r and squar'.' Thar's a buryin' groun', as you know, Mr. Goree, in the yard of yo' old place, under the cedars. Them that lies thar is yo' folks what was killed by the Coltranes. The monyments has the names on 'em. Missis Garvey says a fam'ly buryin' groun' is a sho' sign of quality. She says ef we git the feud, thar's somethin' else ought to go with it. The names on them monyments.is 'Goree,' but they can be changed to ourn by——'

"Go! Go!" screamed Goree, his face turning purple. He stretched out both hands toward the mountaineer, his fingers hooked and shaking. "Go, you ghoul! Even a Ch-Chinaman protects the g-graves of his ancestors—go!"

The squirrel hunter slouched out of the door to his carryall. While he was climbing over the wheel Goree was collecting, with feverish celerity, the money that had fallen from his hand to the floor. As the vehicle slowly turned about, the sheep, with a coat of newly grown wool, was hurrying, in indecent haste, along the path to the courthouse.

At three o'clock in the morning they brought him back to his office, shorn and unconscious. The sheriff, the sportive deputy, the county clerk, and the gay attorney carried him, the chalk-faced man "from the valley" acting as escort.

"On the table," said one of them, and they deposited him there among the litter of his unprofitable books and papers.

"Yance thinks a lot of a pair of deuces when he's liquored up," sighed the sheriff reflectively.

"Too much," said the gay attorney. "A man has no business to play poker who drinks as much as he does. I wonder how much he dropped to-night."

"Close to two hundred. What I wonder is whar he got it. Yance ain't had a cent fur over a month, I know."

"Struck a client, maybe. Well, let's get home before daylight. He'll be all right when he wakes up, except for a sort of beehive about the cranium."

The gang slipped away through the early morning twilight. The next eye to gaze upon the miserable Goree was the orb of day. He peered through the uncurtained window, first deluging the sleeper in a flood of faint gold, but soon pouring upon the mottled red of his flesh a searching, white, summer heat. Goree stirred, half unconsciously, among the table's débris, and turned his face from the window. His movement dislodged a heavy law book, which crashed upon the floor. Opening his eyes, he saw, bending over him, a man in a black frock coat. Locking higher, he discovered a well-worn silk hat, and beneath it the kindly, smooth face of Colonel Abner Coltrane.

A little uncertain of the outcome, the colonel waited for the other to make some sign of recognition. Not in twenty years had male members of these two families faced each other in peace. Goree's eyelids puckered as he strained his blurred sight toward this visitor, and then he smiled serenely.

"Have you brought Stella and Lucy over to play?" he said calmly.

"Do you know me, Yancey?" asked Coltrane.

"Of course I do. You brought me a whip with a whistle in the end."

So he had—twenty-four years ago; when Yancey's father was his best friend.

Goree's eyes wandered about the room. The colonel understood. "Lie still, and I'll bring you some," said he. There was a pump in the yard at the rear, and Goree closed his eyes, listening with rapture to the click of its handle, and the bubbling of the falling stream. Coltrane brought a pitcher of the cool water, and held it for him to drink. Presently Goree sat up—a most forlorn object, his summer suit of flax soiled and crumpled, his discreditable head tousled and unsteady. He tried to wave one of his hands toward the colonel.

"Ex-excuse—everything, will you?" he said. "I must have drunk too much whiskey last night, and gone to bed on the table." His brows knitted into a puzzled frown.

"Out with the boys a while?" asked Coltrane kindly.

"No, I went nowhere. I haven't had a dollar to spend in the last two months. Struck the demijohn too often, I reckon, as usual."

Colonel Coltrane touched him on the shoulder.

"A little while ago, Yancey," he began, "you asked me if I had brought Stella and Lucy over to play. You weren't quite awake then, and must have been dreaming you were a boy again. You are awake now, and I want you to listen to me. I have come from Stella and Lucy to their old playmate, and to my old friend's son. They know that I am going to bring you home with me, and you will find them as ready with a welcome as they were in the old days. I want you to

come to my house and stay until you are
yourself again, and as much longer as you
will. We heard of your being down in the
world, and in the midst of temptation, and
we agreed that you should come over and
play at our house once more. Will you come,
my boy? Will you drop our old family
trouble and come with me?"

"Trouble!" said Goree, opening his eyes
wide. "There was never any trouble between us that I know of. I'm sure we've
always been the best friends. But, good
Lord, Colonel, how could I go to your home
as I am—a drunken wretch, a miserable,
degraded spendthrift and gambler——"

He lurched from the table into his armchair, and began to weep maudlin tears,
mingled with genuine drops of remorse and
shame. Coltrane talked to him persistently
and reasonably, reminding him of the simple
mountain pleasures of which he had once
been so fond, and insisting upon the genuine-
ness of the invitation.

Finally he landed Goree by telling him he
was counting upon his help in the engineering
and transportation of a large amount of felled
timber from a high mountain-side to a water-

way. He knew that Goree had once invented a device for this purpose—a series of slides and chutes—upon which he had justly prided himself. In an instant the poor fellow, delighted at the idea of his being of use to any one, had paper spread upon the table, and was drawing rapid but pitifully shaky lines in demonstration of what he could and would do.

The man was sickened of the husks; his prodigal heart was turning again toward the mountains. His mind was yet strangely clogged, and his thoughts and memories were returning to his brain one by one, like carrier pigeons over a stormy sea. But Coltrane was satisfied with the progress he had made.

Bethel received the surprise of its existence that afternoon when a Coltrane and a Goree rode amicably together through the town. Side by side they rode, out from the dusty streets and gaping townspeople, down across the creek bridge, and up toward the mountain. The prodigal had brushed and washed and combed himself to a more decent figure, but he was unsteady in the saddle, and he seemed to be deep in the contemplation of some vexing problem. Coltrane left him in his mood, relying upon the influence of changed surroundings to restore his equilibrium.

Once Goree was seized with a shaking fit, and almost came to a collapse. He had to dismount and rest at the side of the road. The colonel, foreseeing such a condition, had provided a small flask of whiskey for the journey, but when it was offered to him Goree refused it almost with violence, declaring he would never touch it again. By and by he was recovered, and went quietly enough for a mile or two. Then he pulled up his horse suddenly, and said:

"I lost two hundred dollars last night, playing poker. Now, where did I get that money?"

"Take it easy, Yancey. The mountain air will soon clear it up. We'll go fishing, first thing, at the Pinnacle Falls. The trout are jumping there like bullfrogs. We'll take Stella and Lucy along, and have a picnic on Eagle Rock. Have you forgotten how a hickory-cured-ham sandwich tastes, Yancey, to a hungry fisherman?"

Evidently the colonel did not believe the story of his lost wealth; so Goree retired again into brooding silence.

By late afternoon they had travelled ten of the twelve miles between Bethel and Laurel. Half a mile this side of Laurel lay the old Goree place; a mile or two beyond the village lived the Coltranes. The road was now steep and laborious, but the compensations were many. The tilted aisles of the forest were opulent with leaf and bird and bloom. The tonic air put to shame the pharmacopæia. The glades were dark with mossy shade, and bright with shy rivulets winking from the ferns and laurels. On the lower side they viewed, framed in the near foliage, exquisite sketches of the far valley swooning in its opal haze.

Coltrane was pleased to see that his companion was yielding to the spell of the hills and woods. For now they had but to skirt the base of Painter's Cliff; to cross Elder Branch and mount the hill beyond, and Goree would have to face the squandered home of his fathers. Every rock he passed, every tree, every foot of the roadway, was familiar to him. Though he had forgotten the woods, they thrilled him like the music of "*Home, Sweet Home.*"

They rounded the cliff, descended into

Elder Branch, and paused there to let the horses drink and splash in the swift water. On the right was a rail fence that cornered there, and followed the road and stream. Inclosed by it was the old apple orchard of the home place; the house was yet concealed by the brow of the steep hill. Inside and along the fence, pokeberries, elders, sassafras, and sumac grew high and dense. At a rustle of their branches, both Goree and Coltrane glanced up, and saw a long, yellow, wolfish face above the fence, staring at them with pale, unwinking eyes. The head quickly disappeared; there was a violent swaying of the bushes, and an ungainly figure ran up through the apple orchard in the direction of the house, zigzagging among the trees.

"That's Garvey," said Coltrane; "the man you sold out to. There's no doubt but he's considerably cracked. I had to send him up for moonshining once, several years ago, in spite of the fact that I believed him irresponsible. Why, what's the matter, Yancey?"

Goree was wiping his forehead, and his face had lost its colour. "Do I look queer, too?" he asked, trying to smile. "I'm just remembering a few more things." Some of the alcohol had evaporated from his brain. "I recollect now where I got that two hundred dollars."

"Don't think of it," said Coltrane cheerfully. "Later on we'll figure it all out together."

They rode out of the branch, and when they reached the foot of the hill Goree stopped again.

"Did you ever suspect I was a very vain kind of fellow, Colonel?" he asked. "Sort of foolish proud about appearances?"

The colonel's eyes refused to wander to the soiled, sagging suit of flax and the faded slouch hat.

"It seems to me," he replied, mystified, but humouring him, "I remember a young buck about twenty, with the tightest coat, the sleekest hair, and the prancingest saddle horse in the Blue Ridge."

"Right you are," said Goree eagerly. "And it's in me yet, though it don't show. Oh, I'm as vain as a turkey gobbler, and as proud as Lucifer. I'm going to ask you to indulge this weakness of mine in a little matter."

"Speak out, Yancey. We'll create you Duke of Laurel and Baron of Blue Ridge, if you choose; and you shall have a feather out of Stella's peacock's tail to wear in your hat."

"I'm in earnest. In a few minutes we'll pass the house up there on the hill where I was born, and where my people have lived for nearly a century. Strangers live there now—and look at me! I am about to show myself to them ragged and poverty-stricken, a wastrel and a beggar. Colonel Coltrane, I'm ashamed to do it. I want you to let me wear your coat and hat until we are out of sight beyond. I know you think it a foolish pride, but I want to make as good a showing as I can when I pass the old place."

"Now, what does this mean?" said Coltrane to himself, as he compared his companion's sane looks and quiet demeanour with his strange request. But he was already unbuttoning the coat, assenting readily, as if the fancy were in no wise to be considered strange.

The coat and hat fitted Goree well. He buttoned the former about him with a look of satisfaction and dignity. He and Coltrane were nearly the same size—rather tall, portly, and erect. Twenty-five years were between them, but in appearance they might have been brothers. Goree looked older than his age; his face was puffy and lined; the colonel had the smooth, fresh complexion of a temperate liver. He put on Goree's disreputable old flax coat and faded slouch hat.

"Now," said Goree, taking up the reins, "I'm all right. I want you to ride about ten feet in the rear as we go by, Colonel, so that they can get a good look at me. They'll see I'm no back number yet, by any means. I guess I'll show up pretty well to them once more, anyhow. Let's ride on."

He set out up the hill at a smart trot, the colonel following, as he had been requested.

Goree sat straight in the saddle, with head erect, but his eyes were turned to the right, sharply scanning every shrub and fence and hiding-place in the old homestead yard. Once he muttered to himself, "Will the crazy fool try it, or did I dream half of it?"

It was when he came opposite the little family burying ground that he saw what he had been looking for—a puff of white smoke coming from the thick cedars in one corner. He toppled so slowly to the left that Coltrane had time to urge his horse to that side, and catch him with one arm.

The squirrel hunter had not overpraised

his aim. He had sent the bullet where he intended, and where Goree had expected that it would pass—through the breast of Colonel Abner Coltrane's black frock coat.

Goree leaned heavily against Coltrane, but he did not fall. The horses kept pace, side by side, and the colonel's arm kept him steady. The little white houses of Laurel shone through the trees, half a mile away. Goree reached out one hand and groped until it rested upon Coltrane's fingers, which held his bridle.

"Good friend," he said, and that was all.

Thus did Yancey Goree, as he rode past his old home, make, considering all things, the best showing that was in his power.

THE END